CONTRITE

by

KATHY
COOPMANS

© 2015

To Yamara, Karrie, and Heather.
Always remember that if you fall, I will be there to pick you up.

Chapter One

I'm standing in the Atlanta Airport fidgeting and pacing back and forth as I wait for my husband Turner to come walking through the gate. It's been a week since I have seen him; to some that may not be a long time, but to me it's been forever. This is the longest we have been apart since we started dating in our sophomore year of college. Both of us were studying to be accountants and now we have our own small firm in a small town on the outskirts of Atlanta.

Usually when Turner goes away on a business trip I go with him. However, my brother Zack and his wife Krista just had their first child- my handsome nephew, Nolan. I had to be there for his birth. I couldn't miss seeing my brother's first child come into this world, and I am so glad I didn't. The look on Zack's face when he showed Nolan to me from the nursery window is one I will never forget. It was a moment of pride for my entire family, one I simply cannot describe.

My dad stood beside me with tears of happiness welling openly as he observed my brother holding his son. When Nolan was placed in my father's arms for the first time, I cried right along with him as he cooed at the baby.

I have never seen my dad cry, not even when my bitch of a mother left us all ten years ago to move on to bigger and better things . . . her words, not mine. Zack and I haven't talked to her in two years.

She showed up one day on my doorstep. I freaked the hell out when I answered the door and there she stood, draped in diamonds and some fancy designer dress, pulling me in for a hug like we were best friends. Turner hated her, and to this day I still don't know why she was there. To brag about how she was happily married to some guy with lots of money, I suppose.

She went on and on about how happy she was, how she missed us all so much, and how she made a mistake by leaving us. She said she wanted to start over. I told her there was no chance in hell that I wanted anything whatsoever to do with her.

When Turner asked her to leave and never come back again, she fake cried all the way to the damn door. Now we have no idea where she is, not that she was around much, anyway. She should be the poster child for the worst mother. No, I take that back. She *is* the worst mother. But today is all about the man who I call 'my world.'

I shiver just thinking about him and how much I have missed him. Turner Calloway stole my breath away eight years ago when he walked into class and sat down right next to me. I was the shy, timid nerd girl who just wanted to be happy and to make my father proud.

After my mother left, I took care of my dad and brother the best way I knew how, cooking, cleaning, and doing everything else my selfish mother should have been doing. Dad and Zack were constantly riding my ass about going out and doing something. I never wanted to. Sure, I had friends, and they usually came over to my house. I just didn't want my dad to ever be alone. I went to school and came home, and even when I went to college, I still lived at home. Dad tried to convince me I needed to get out and experience college life. Nope. Not me. I just wasn't interested, until the day I laid eyes on Turner.

After two weeks of talking back and forth to each other in class, he finally got me to give him my number, and we've been together ever since. My dad about shit himself and practically shoved me out the door when I finally told him about Turner. Instead of being the typical dad who claims no man is good enough for his daughter, my dad was the opposite. He fell in love with Turner just as I did.

My older brother Zack? Not so much. He's only older by eighteen months but he acts as if it's a decade. He grilled Turner and even threatened to kick his ass once if he ever hurt me.

Turner's response was, "Dude, I have a woman worth spoiling. For years she was yours to protect and now she's mine, so back the fuck off."

That was all it took to win Zack over, and the two of them have been best friends ever since.

Heaving a heavy sigh, I keep my eyes on the doors of the terminal and wait for them to open. All I want to do is leap over all these people and into the arms of my man.

Finally, the doors open. I can already feel his arms wrapped around me and his lips moving reverently against mine as I get lost in handsome, green-eyed, dark-haired Turner Calloway.

I freeze on the spot when I see him walking toward me. When he lifts his head and scans the area, his eyes land on mine, and the crooked smile that made me fall in love with him is where my eyes stay focused.

His pace quickens and he approaches me with a lethal stare. I can't help but smile back.

"Jesus Christ. I fucking missed you so damn bad."

He scoops me up in his arms and twirls me around, burying his face into my long, blonde hair.

"I missed you too, lover boy," I reply, smiling as he keeps his head buried in my hair.

"You smell so damn good, Clove," Turner whispers softly in my ear. "Let's get the hell out of here so I can get a proper welcome home from my wife. Shall we?"

Turner gives me that crooked smile as he places me back down on the floor.

"Sounds good to me," I say, knowing exactly what Turner has in mind for us when we get home.

I cannot think of one time where my husband has not worshipped either all or some part of my body before we made love. Sure, he likes to fuck hard and fast, but not before he makes me squirm or beg for him to take me after his skilled hands and mouth have had their fill of whichever body part of mine he is fascinated with at the time.

"Tell me again why we live in a big city?"

Turner's tension fills the air of our small luxury SUV. I lean my head back against the headrest and reach over and run my hand through his hair to try and ease his stress as we sit in bumper-to-bumper afternoon traffic. I have always loved the color of his hair. It's somewhere between brown and black, and so thick.

"That's enough, Clove."

Turner startles me, jerking his head so I have no other choice but to drop my hand. He's gone from night to day in a nanosecond.

"Chill out, Turner. God. We drive in this every day. What's got you so wound up, anyway? You love it when I run my hands through your hair."

He just lets out a small huff as he rubs his hands up and down his face.

"Look, I'm sorry, okay? It's just the last thing I want to do after flying across the damn country is to sit in this damn car. I just want to get you home and get you underneath me."

He brings his hand over and skims underneath my shorts as he runs his hand along the seam of my panties.

"Open your legs for me, Clove," he says seductively, keeping one hand on the steering wheel and his eyes on the road as the traffic starts to move.

My legs willingly open and he rubs across my aching sex. I long for him to touch me. All my agitation flies out the damn window when I see the hunger in my husband's eyes.

I've only been thinking of myself and how much I have missed him, never thinking of the fact that he missed me, too.

"Pull your shorts down and let me see that beautiful cunt of yours," he demands, and I whip my head around and look at him in shock because he knows I hate that word.

"Turner, why would you say that?" I push my legs back together but he doesn't remove his hand.

"Shit. I don't know what's gotten into me. All I know is that I missed you like fucking crazy and if I don't touch you soon, I am going to fucking explode over here. Please pull those shorts down and let me touch you," he whispers.

I have no idea why my sweet, caring husband has been a damn cranky bastard since we left the airport. He rarely ever raises his voice to me, let alone uses the one word in front of me I absolutely despise. That "C" word is about the most degrading word I have ever heard.

Maybe he's just as irritated about our separation as I am and jet lag is starting to kick in. I don't know what his problem is. Turner has never been one to hide his feelings about anything, especially with me.

I shimmy my shorts and black lace panties down my long legs. Good Lord. For the first time since we bought this fancy vehicle I am thankful for the dark windows as I sit here splayed out naked from the waist down in the middle of the afternoon on a busy interstate in downtown Atlanta. It does give me a little bit of a thrill doing something we have never done before.

"God damn, baby, I am one lucky son of a bitch. That pussy is so damn beautiful."

I gasp as he cups me completely and he starts running his hand all over the top of my freshly waxed core.

"So smooth."

His voice is getting ragged and the pleasure of him rubbing me starts to speed up my heart rate as I close my eyes and squirm lower in my seat.

"You missed me, didn't you my love?"

I know he is talking but I am too caught in up what his hand is doing to my body as he slowly continues to take his fingers and draw small patterns across my skin. I moan as he reaches the petals of my lips. Being teased like this is torture like you would not believe.

"Yes, Turner," I practically scream as his hand surely but steadily floats its way down to brush across my nether lips. He wastes no time, sliding his fingers up and down and tracing the edges, teasing and causing me to moan and beg him to put his fingers inside.

"Damn, Clove. I can feel how wet you are. You need to get off, babe? Do you want me to plunge my fingers inside this sweet smelling pussy? This car is full of the smell of your arousal. I am so fucking hard over here right now that if I wasn't in such a big hurry to get you in our bed and pound the ever-loving shit out of you, I would pull over right now and fuck you so hard you would know I have been there every time you walk for the next damn week."

His deep, throaty words bring me out of the dream I was having of Turner and his magic hands. Before I can say anything about how his dirty talk has me so turned on, he pinches my clit and tugs so hard that the pain actually causes pleasure to run through my entire body. I scream his name but he doesn't stop the torture at all; he continues to rub me until I know I am drenched.

"You are going to be so much fun to fuck, my receptive wife. Do you like this, Clove?" he questions as he brutally slides his finger inside.

I clamp down and wiggle to try and get him to plunge in deeper. I have never been very verbal when we make love, but I quickly toss that aside.

My husband starts sliding his finger in and out, getting me wetter than I have been in a very long time.

"Oh, God." I arch my back and press my hips into his hand harder.

"Hell, yeah. Give me that orgasm, babe. Let me have it all over my finger. I am dying to taste you. You like me finger fucking you and having your sweet smelling pussy all over my fingers?"

"God, yes," I moan.

"Don't come for me yet, babe, we're almost home."

I barely register what he is saying to me as he continues on with his blissful torture.

All of a sudden I feel the loss of his fingers and I open my eyes as I notice we are pulling into the garage of our two-story Cape Cod style home. Turner cuts the engine and the garage door closes behind us and I look over at him in the semi-dark. His hands are gripping the steering wheel and he exhales noisily, turning his head and looking at me with a burning blaze of fire and desire in his eyes.

I squirm in my seat. I have never seen my husband look at me like that before and for some reason, it turns me on. I feel myself becoming even wetter with desire for him to touch me again. As if he knows exactly what I am thinking, he loosens his grip on the steering wheel and gets out of the car. I watch him round the front of the car like a predator that is ready to kill his prey. He swings my car door open and painfully grabs my legs, swinging them around as he kneels onto the garage floor.

He yanks me straight into his face. Half of my ass is hanging off the seat and my head falls back against the console with a thud. I scream as he throws my legs over his shoulders and buries his tongue deeply inside me.

My back arches and my legs start to shake as he starts out with slow, hard strokes and then speeds up gradually. I grind my aching flesh into his face. He has never gone down on me like this before.

"Oh, Jesus. Turner. God, yes. More!" I pant. I am just on the cusp of coming when he pulls his face off of me.

"You want more, Clove? I'll give you more. I am going to make you come like you have never come before. Now come all over my fucking face, sweet girl."

Jesus Christ. I am gone when he sticks his tongue back into my opening and swirls it around against my walls. After he licks and sucks me to the best orgasm he has ever given me, he doesn't stop. He nips at my clit with his teeth over and over while he shoves two fingers inside me, curving them upward to hit the spot that has me screaming and begging him to give me the release I so desperately need.

My clit feels like it is turning inside out and my pussy is clenching wildly. I come for the second time, and I don't even recognize my own voice as I scream my husband's name so loud, it's piercing even to my own ears.

I instantly feel his loss as he places my legs down. When I start to become more alert, I open my eyes and gape at the beast of a man who is staring down at my glistening pussy.

He's observing it as if it's the first time he has ever seen it.

"So beautiful. Christ Almighty, this is all mine. Keep them spread, Clove. I am far from done with you," he rasps.

He pops open the button of his jeans and unzips them, then pulls them down along with his boxers. His incredible cock pulses, looking even bigger than I remember, and it's only been a week. I observe every part of his glorious body, taking in every inch of what has got to be the most finely chiseled piece of perfection. My desire is to touch him, but as I reach my hand up to familiarize myself with the sex god standing before me, he takes a small step back, barely out of my reach.

"You want this, Clove?" Turner asks as he strokes himself. "You want me to fuck that tight, sweet pussy of yours or do you want me to fuck that hot mouth?"

I gulp and stare up at the man who I know is my husband, yet seems different in the few short hours since he has been home. Even though I want to take him in my mouth, I spread my legs even farther, which seems to be enough of an answer for him. He lets go of himself and bends down, taking his shoes off along with his pants and briefs, and scoops me out of the vehicle. He slams the door shut and sits down on a workbench with me still wrapped tightly around him.

Without any warning at all he grabs his dick and slams inside me so hard, my head falls back. I swear to everything holy I black out for a second, but I am instantly awakened as my husband drives his massive cock into me like this is the first or the last time he is ever going to have me. I thrust my pelvis back and forth and grind down on him as hard as I can while clenching his dick the best way I know how.

We have never before had sex so animalistic. I tilt my head back and groan. In response, he grabs my thin t-shirt and rips it right down the middle, then unhooks the front clasp of my bra allowing my heavy, aching breasts to hang free. He cups one in his big hand and brings his mouth down on the other, sucking on my already pebbled nipple while biting down and then pinching my other nipple in between his fingers.

"Oh, fuck! I am going to come, Turner. God, I am going to explode all over you!"

Releasing my breast from his mouth, he brings his lips to mine and ravishes me with a brutal kiss. Our tongues and teeth clash, and I scream his name into his mouth as I come all over him. Within seconds, he heaves himself up into me as far as he can get then stills us both as I feel his warm juice spill inside me.

We are both breathing so damn hard it takes us several minutes to be able to calm down. Turner has always been such a careful lover, always tender and putting my needs before his own, but this was definitely the best sex I have ever had.

I sit here and stare into the eyes of my handsome husband and really look at him. Even though he made sure to satisfy me more than he has ever done before, now I cannot help but wonder what in the hell happened to my gentle Turner while he was gone. The man staring back at me doesn't look like the same man who left me a week ago.

No. This man has a blank expression on his face; his eyes are as vacant as they come.

Chapter Two

"Turner?" I ask softly. "Is something wrong?"

His brows furrow as his eyes bore heavily into mine, mystified. I quickly climb off of him, instantly feeling the loss of his connection. That must be what finally snaps him out of his stupor.

"Fuck! Clove, baby. I am so damn sorry."

I watch my loving and caring husband put his face in his hands and his shoulders sag. I sit down next to him on the bench and place my hand on his shoulder.

"Talk to me," I say tenderly. He lifts his head slightly.

"It seems like all I have ever done since you picked me up is say sorry. But I am sorry, Clove. I didn't mean to take you so roughly."

His eyes plead with mine as he looks at me.

"Turner." I place my hand on his chin to hold his gaze to mine. "Did you hear me complaining? I loved it, honey. Rough, smooth, slow, fast. It doesn't matter to me. That just showed me exactly how much you missed me." I nudge his shoulder slightly. "Don't ever apologize for wanting to take me like that ever again."

We sit in silence for several minutes before he stands up and retrieves my shorts and panties out of the car and hands them to me along with my flip-flops. Then he picks his jeans and boxers up off of the garage floor and pulls them on, leaving the top button of his jeans open. With a smirk on his face, he takes a few steps toward me.

"So you liked it rough like that?" He reaches out and pulls me close to him. I place my hands on his strong, sturdy chest.

"I did," I whisper.

"I did, too. Thank you for forgiving me for my little space out a few minutes ago. It's just . . . God, Clove. If I ever did anything to hurt you, I would never be able to forgive myself."

"I am not some fragile flower who is going to wilt and die if you hold and squeeze it too hard, Turner, so quit beating yourself up. I actually loved welcoming you home in that way."

I lay my head on his chest and listen to the steady beat of his heart, but the tone of his voice when he said he would never be able to forgive himself makes me think that Turner is trying to convince himself of that fact more than he is trying to convince me.

****

"So tell me about this conference? Was it boring?" I question Turner as we are eating dinner.

"Fuck, yes, it was boring. I hate those damn things and you know it. The state has made a few changes but not anything we can't go over at work tomorrow," he says as he knocks back another beer.

I've lost count. He drank three in less than an hour while I was making dinner. Turner usually has a beer or two a few times a week; maybe more if we go out on a date or with our friends, but nothing like this. And he's hardly eaten any of his dinner. It's his mom's fried chicken recipe, his favorite. He usually devours everything on his plate and most times goes back for more.

I'm not paying attention to a word he is saying as I sit there listening to him drone on and on about the conference he went to. I use the time to study him covertly. It's not big things, but subtle changes in his mannerisms that for some reason have put me on edge, like how he gestures certain ways with his hands. And, not one time since we have sat down has he looked at me when he speaks.

Panic starts to set in and I try not to let it show. Is he hiding something from me, or am I just paranoid because we have been away from each other for the first time?

I don't know what to make of his strange behavior. Is he having an affair? Oh, God. No, please don't let that be it. I watch him get up and put his half-eaten plate into the sink and pull another beer out from the fridge. He slams the door shut with his foot and I jump from the sound.

"I didn't mean to scare you, love," he says as he walks up behind me and cups one of my breasts in his hand. I feel his warm, beer-scented breath against my neck. "You ready for round two, Clove?"

He pinches my nipple between his fingers and it stings. What is up with that? It's not that the pinching hurts so much; it actually feels good mixing a little pain with the pleasure. It's just, that's not what he does. Turner loves to bring my breasts to his mouth and suck until he has them nice and hard, and then he likes to run his hands over the top of the hard peaks.

My mind just isn't focused on sex right now, I guess. I have never turned my husband down when he wants it, but I'll be damned if I am going to have sex with him right now. He just doesn't seem like himself.

All these dark and gloomy thoughts run through my head. Night and day. Black and white. I sneak a peek at him through my lashes. Yup, I'm pretty sure this is the same man I dropped off at the airport a week ago, I joke darkly to myself. So why is he acting so strangely? I turn my head away from him and pick up my plate to take it to the sink.

"I need to clean up the kitchen. Why don't you go relax in the living room and find a movie to put on? I'll be in shortly and we can watch before we go to bed."

"Yeah, that sounds like a good idea. Let me just grab another beer and I'll get out of your way."

He walks past me and I watch him like a motherfucking hawk. My husband is hiding something from me, and I am going to dig around until I find out exactly what it is.

Fifteen minutes. Just fifteen damn minutes is all I spend in the kitchen, and by the time I walk into the living room, Turner is lounging on the couch watching a ball game, all thoughts of our movie night apparently erased from his memory.

I watch him covertly from behind the sofa as he lies on his back staring at the screen. Am I being paranoid? I have no clue what has happened to my husband, but the thought of him being with another woman has my gut twisted and my heart breaking.

I have given my all to this man. Is he cheating on me? And why? We're together all the time. Turner dotes on me. He's romantic; he's kind. I have so many questions. I can't just come out and ask him. I love him so much that I know I wouldn't be able to survive a blow like that. It would destroy me.

"Oh, Turner . . . my world, my love. What in the hell is going on?" I whisper.

I continue to stare at the man who owns my heart and think back to the sex we had in the garage. The feeling of pure, raw, primal fucking is what has me shuddering and aching between my legs.

Turner has never been like that with me before. Not one time has he talked to me the way he did today. I am not going to lie by saying I didn't enjoy the dirty talk, but shit! When he said *cunt*, I have to admit I was a little shocked . . . no, I was more like stunned, at his language.

Turner is not boring by any means. I quiver at the memory of the things he can do with his tongue. Today, he dove right in, as usual. One thing I can say about my husband is that he has a huge appetite for sex, always has. What I don't understand is why it was so rough. Not that I didn't like it, because I did.

It was the best sex we have ever had, hands down. So intense, like neither one of us could get enough of the other. I have never seen Turner come apart like that. The wild side of me that I never even knew I had wants more of that kind of sex. I would love for Turner to take me any way he wants me, to pound into me over and over again until I am so sore that I can barely walk the next day.

A single tear slowly falls down my face as I envision another woman touching, kissing, and making love to my husband. The pain is too much to bear.

I need to stop thinking this way; there is absolutely no way that Turner would destroy everything we have and the future we've planned. Children, grandchildren . . . I refuse to believe it. He would never cheat on me. Turner Calloway is an honest man. Why have these thoughts even popped into my head in the first place?

I tilt my head to the side as I run my hand through my hair and then place it over my heart. It's beating so damn fast. I've never had a panic attack before, but this sure as hell feels like one. I am overwhelmed by the fear-inducing unknown as my heart races, pounding relentlessly in my chest. I start to hyperventilate, feeling as if I could throw up at any moment.

I scurry backwards out of the room as fast as I can before Turner even realizes I was there. Upon entering the kitchen I bend over the sink, trying to regain my composure. I breathe in and out several times to calm myself down and my heart rate gradually returns to normal.

The quicker I get these ludicrous ideas out of my head, the quicker I can get back to the happy woman I was when I left here to pick him up. I know this, so why do I have the nagging sensation deep in the pit of my stomach that I should investigate a little further?

I push away from the sink and on silent feet go to grab Turner's carry-on bag from where he left it by the front door.

I rush down the hall to the laundry room with it and set it on the small table I use to fold laundry. My husband is in the habit of leaving loose change and receipts in his pockets, so I carefully check each one. As I am pulling out a pair of jeans, a card falls to the floor.

"The Cigar Bar," it reads.

What in the hell would he have this for? He hates the smell of cigars with a passion. Just when I thought I'd pushed my insecurities to the back of my mind, I find this. I don't understand at all what's happening here. My brain is short-circuiting and I need someone to hit the reset button. I grab the edge of the washing machine to steady myself, but I feel like all I am doing is stumbling over a cliff. The card slips through my fingers and falls to the floor as I press the heels of my hands into my eyes.

My legs give out and I slide down to the floor, shaking my head back and forth as pain rips through my chest. Am I reading too much into this? Maybe Turner was tired from his trip and just needed to unwind and relax. Damn it all to hell, my head is spinning and I feel like I am about to lose control.

"It's only a couple of strange things, Clove. Why are you letting this get to you?" I say out loud.

I think for a moment about those words, but you know what? I know my husband. There is no fucking way he would go to a cigar bar, and there is no fucking way he would sit around and drink the way he did tonight . . . unless there was something very, very, wrong.

Fuck me, I am going to find out. But how? There's no one I can share this with; they would all laugh in my face and think I am being ridiculous. Most of my friends are jealous of the way Turner treats me. Even after all of these years, he still opens my car door for me, and kisses me goodnight and good morning.

So many times I have seen this man looking at me with simple adoration. Every single time I catch him at it, we have a routine. 'Why are you looking at me like that?' I'll ask him. And his answer is invariably, 'I'm admiring the most beautiful woman in the world. Is that all right with you?' 'It's always all right with me,' I smile.

But not today. Every time he looked at me today, all I saw was a man who looked like he had never seen me before.

Damn. What is wrong with me and my crazy thoughts? I rub my temples and try to think. Knowing the truth would be so much better than this torture, so I pick up the phone and send a text to the one person who I know will listen to me. My brother, Zack.

I text him, telling him I really need to talk to him. I sit my phone on the floor next to me and wait on his reply. After a few moments, he texts back.

> Are you all right?
> Yeah, fine. I just need to talk to you about something is all.
> All right. Call me tomorrow. Night, and love you, sis.
> Love you, too. Give my little nephew a big kiss from me.
> :)

A chuckle escapes my lips at his smiley face, but all too soon my thoughts drift back to Turner. Straightening up, I tell myself that even though his behavior is a little strange, there are not sufficient signs of an affair, though the evidence certainly seems to point to one.

I scoop the card up off of the floor and slip it back into his bag, and try and put his clothes back inside exactly the way they were. I set it back where he left it. Fuck it; he can clean the damn thing out himself.

My mind is jumping all over the place like a damn flea. I need to calm down and pull myself together before I face Turner again.

I am going to push all of this into the back of my mind until I have proof of my suspicions. The best way to find out the truth is to throw him off guard by acting as if his actions haven't affected me at all.

I should just go upstairs to our room without saying anything and let him come to bed whenever he wants. Yeah, right. He would definitely know something is wrong, then. Our relationship doesn't work that way. We never go to bed mad at each other, and we never go to sleep without telling each other good night, so I have to pretend everything is fine and not like every part of my body is shattered and broken. I take a deep breath. Even though I want to cry and break down right here on my living room floor, I can't, and I won't. I keep telling myself over and over to be strong.

"Turner."

I tenderly touch his arm. He blinks a few times but his eyes stay riveted on the game.

"Hey. What time is it?" he asks tiredly.

"It's ten-thirty and I thought our bed would be more comfortable than the couch. We can finish watching the game in bed, if you would like?"

His next words take me by surprise, casting a shadow of a doubt over the possible affair.

"Yes, Mrs. Calloway. Our bed is much more comfortable than this couch. I missed waking up and having you cradled in my arms. Every time I look at you, I can't believe that you're mine."

He then reaches up and caresses my check with his hand and of course I lean into it. I have missed his sweet, gentle touch.

"I missed you so much, Turner."

I reach my hand out for him to take and we head upstairs hand in hand to get ready for bed.

Hearing the sounds of his heavy breathing as I drift to sleep brings images of him doing this exact same thing with someone else. I will be damned if another woman takes what is mine. One thing is for certain. If he is having an affair, I will fucking kill both of them.

****

There is nothing like the feeling of caffeine coursing through my veins after a bad night's sleep. My mind went off on a tangent last night when we climbed into bed. After Turner said those sweet things to me, he took care of his business in the bathroom and fell right to sleep the minute his head hit the pillow. He never does that, and I mean, EVER. He has never gone to bed without kissing me goodnight or pulling me close to him. Sure, we have slept without spooning or cuddling, but never like this.

All these tormenting thoughts I had throughout the night had me getting up and taking this damn cigar card back out of his suitcase. As I sit here twirling it between my fingers, I keep wondering to myself if I am just reading something into all this that's not there. One minute I am thinking there is no fucking way he would do this to me, and the next minute, BAM! I am second-guessing myself.

I hear the shower turn off indicating that Turner is done, so I stuff the card into the pocket of my black silk robe and go pour my husband a cup of coffee. He strolls into the kitchen with only a towel wrapped around his waist. His body is lightly toned and his strong, square jaw has a few days of dark scruff. I could eat him for breakfast, but as I watch him make his way into the kitchen, I banish those thoughts as quickly as they come. The thought of another woman having her hands all over what has only ever been mine makes me tremble.

"Good morning, Clove." Graciously he puts his arms around me and kisses me softly on my lips. "You okay, sweetheart? You're shaking."

A look of concern crosses his face and he furrows his brows. Snapping out of my funk, I muster a smile and lean forward and kiss him back.

"I'm fine, lover boy. I missed seeing you wandering around in just a towel in the morning, so I was admiring my view."

My words must have an effect on him. I feel him growing hard and thick under the towel as he presses himself into me. *Not today, buddy*, I think to myself. He glances at the clock on the stove and then back to me.

"Shit. As much as I would love to take you back to bed and make slow, sweet, torturous love to you, we have to get our asses to the office so you can catch me up on what I missed."

I remove my hands from his chest as he steps away from me and starts to leave the kitchen. He pauses on the threshold and turns back around. I think he is going to say something to me, but instead he eyes his carryon bag which is sitting right by the door where he left it. Oh fuck. My eyes go wide as he walks over and picks it up.

"Hurry your sexy ass up so we can beat this fucking morning traffic, Clove."

My mouth gapes wide open as I eyeball him walking past me and right up the stairs as if everything were normal.

"Who are you and what have you done with my husband?" I mutter under my breath.

My mouth is still hanging open as we make the thirty minute drive to work and Turner acts as if nothing is wrong. I'm angrier than a swarm of bees. I cannot wait to get away from him this morning.

I close the door to my office and wait for the opportunity to call the only person who I trust enough to confide in. My brother.

Chapter Three

I do take my job seriously, but today I cannot put a damned thing into perspective as I sit here and go over the e-mail that Turner sent me with details about his conference. Instead, I sit here tapping my pencil on my desk and checking the clock every minute waiting for Turner to let me know he is heading to lunch with a client so I can call Zack. I place my elbows on my desk and rub my temples, trying to alleviate some of the tension. There is a slight knock on my door. I lift my head just as Turner walks in.

"Hey, babe. You all right?"

"Yeah. I'm fine," I snap.

"You sure? You seem a little off this morning."

"I'm sure, babe. You heading out for your lunch meeting?"

He doesn't meet my eyes. If I hadn't set this meeting up myself, I would think he was lying. He is looking everywhere but at me. Like a good little wife, I stand up and walk around my desk and wrap my arms around his neck. When I reach him, he pulls me into his chest.

"I'll be back in a few hours or so, okay?"

"Okay. I'm going to keep going over this stuff you sent me and then I need to do some monthly reports, so have a good lunch."

Turner surprises the shit out of me when he leans down and takes my mouth in a fiery kiss that has my senses on overload. His tongue demands entrance into my mouth and even though I have all these fears inside of me, I cannot help but kiss him back. We both start breathing heavily as our tongues twine together. He pulls my waist even tighter into him and I feel what this kiss is doing to him. It's doing the same to me. I feel the ache stirring between my legs.

"Holy fucking shit. Do I have to go to this fucking meeting?" Turner asks as he adjusts himself through his pants.

"Um. Yes, you do, but I will be waiting right here for you when you get back," I lie. The minute he leaves, I am praying like hell that I can call Zack and tell him my suspicions.

"All right, then. We'll finish this when I get back." He places a small kiss on my cheek. "Do you want me to bring you anything back? A salad or something?"

"I'm good. I can go across the street to the deli in a few. Now go before you're late."

I shoo him out of my office and listen to him grumble something about a bossy wife. I chuckle and then shut my door leaning my back up against it. I am proud of myself for the way I handled him. I bring my hand to my lips, softly pressing them, and close my eyes to relish the feel of how good his kisses are. But as hard as I try, I can't hold back the vision of Turner with someone else. I can't. My eyes fly open and on wobbly legs I make my way over to my desk to call my brother.

"Hey, sis." Zack picks up on the first ring.

"Hey. How's my handsome nephew?"

"He is so perfect, Clove. He's taken to breastfeeding like a champ and makes the cutest little faces. I just can't wait to do all that cool ass father and son stuff, you know?"

I am beaming with pride and happiness for my brother as I sit here and listen to him. I hate to tell him my qualms about Turner, but with him being a cop, I know he has the connections to help me find out what the hell is going on.

"So, how was Turner's trip? Boring as fuck I bet," he chuckles.

"Whatever, bro. He said it went well. Actually, Turner is the reason why I am calling."

"What's going on?"

He must hear the uneasiness in my voice with the sharp way he responds.

Taking a deep breath, I lean back in my chair and tell him everything that has happened since my husband has returned home . . . not going into too much detail about the sex, but just enough to let him know that it was different than any other time before.

"Shit, Clove. That doesn't sound like Turner at all. You sure you're not reading the signs wrong? I mean, hell, you two have never been apart like this before. Maybe he was just tired and couldn't wait to get home."

I shake my head back and forth even though I know he cannot see me.

"No," I state a little too loudly. "I am telling you that something is not right, Zack. I know my husband better than anyone else, and he is not acting right. Something is off. I don't know why I think he's having an affair . . . maybe that's not it, but something is definitely not right with him. I- I'm so scared. I just can't lose him. Not like this. And especially not to another woman." Tears start to rapidly flow down my cheeks.

"Hey. Come on, now. Don't start crying. There has to be a logical explanation for all of this, and you know it. Like I said before, I just can't see Turner cheating on you, Clove. That man loves you, and you know it. You're overreacting here. There is just no way."

I try and process what he is saying and I know he knows Turner, but shit, I know him better. I know when something is off with him and there is. I can feel it. Every part of my body feels it.

"I'll tell you what, why don't you tell him when he gets back that I invited you guys over for dinner tonight for him to meet Nolan, and I will feel him out and see what I think?"

I take a deep breath and let it out.

"Okay. Sure. I would love to see my little nephew myself, anyway. What time should we come over? Oh, wait. Are you sure Krista is up for company? I mean, she did just have a baby a week ago, you know. I am sure she is exhausted."

"We're both exhausted, sis, but not enough that I can't have my sister over for a few hours. Besides, I will stop and pick up a couple pizzas on the way. She'll be fine with it."

"Well, if you're sure then yes, I would love that. Oh, and Zack? Please don't say anything about this to dad. You know how he worries all the damn time."

My face grows sadder as I think about my father and how much he worries about the two of us.

"I won't say anything to anyone, Clove, not even Krista. I have a feeling that everything is fine and you're just being paranoid over nothing. I should be home by five, so why don't you two just come over straight from work, okay?"

"Sounds good. Thank you, Zack."

"Hey, anything for you and you know that. Now get back to work crunching stupid ass numbers or whatever the hell it is that you do."

Forcing a small smile, I hang up with my brother and feel a little bit lighter about the situation after talking to him. Yet that doubt still lingers, and frankly it scares me to death.

A few hours later, I am knee-deep in reports when I hear Turner outside of my door talking to our secretary, Mandy. I look up from the pile of papers on my desk just in time to see him strut through my door.

"How did it go?"

"It went good. Really good. We got the job!" he smiles enthusiastically.

"That's great, Turner! Nice job."

"Well, I wouldn't give myself all the credit, Clove. You seemed to impress them just as much as I did. Even more so, I think." He quirks his eyebrow.

"What's that supposed to mean?"

"It doesn't mean anything. I just believe you won them over before I had a chance to. Are you upset with me about something? Is it about last night? I thought I apologized for my behavior."

"No, I'm fine. Exhausted, I guess. I didn't sleep very well when you were gone and I think it's all catching up to me now," I lie.

Making his way over to my desk, he stands behind me and gently starts to rub my shoulders with his big, strong hands.

"You're so tense."

"Mmhmm," is all I can seem to get out as I let myself relax under his touch.

His hands caress and massage my flesh and it feels so good. When his hands start to roam lower, that is when my body seems to tense up again as he dips his hand inside my gray silk blouse.

"The door is open, Turner. What if Mandy walks in?"

"Who cares if she walks in, Clove? We're married, for fuck's sake, and if I want to feel my wife up in her office then I can." He bends down and nips the side of my neck as he pinches my nipples through my lacy bra. "God, I love how your tits feel in my hands. You're so fucking perfect and I can't wait to bury my dick inside that tight pussy that belongs to me."

Both of our breathing becomes ragged as he pinches and tugs my nipples. I have lost all reason and control of my body with his touch. When my toes start to curl and my body starts twisting with desire, and I start to writhe from the pure onslaught of his seduction, that's when he stops and spins me around in my chair. My look shoots daggers up at him in frustration.

"You asshole! You start that and don't finish? Now I *am* pissed off at you."

"No you're not, because you know I'll finish the job later. There is no way in hell that you're going to come without me being able to lick up every last drop of your sweet self. Now get your ass back to work and let's be out of here by five and go grab something to eat somewhere."

"Oh! I almost forgot! I talked to Zack and he invited us over for some pizza so you could meet Nolan tonight after work. I told him it was okay."

"Um. Sure. All right. But only for a few hours, all right? I need to finish what I just started, and I would prefer to have my wife naked and squirming underneath me in our bed while my dick slides into your perfect pussy as it commands me to fuck you."

He stares down at me with hunger in his eyes.

"I would love that, too."

He bends down and gives me a chaste kiss and spins my chair back around.

"I love you, Clove," he says as he walks out the door.

Fuck me if I am not more confused than ever right now. The man that was just in here was the attentive husband I remember, with his long, strong fingers. His penetrating, intent look said he only sees me.

And yet, his mouth . . . his filthy damn mouth has my core convulsing with need and a desperate ache for him to march his ass right back in here and fuck me right here on my desk.

But even though the lower half of my body enjoyed his dirty talk, the upper half that holds my heart is desperate to know why the hell his unfamiliar, foul words leave me with such desire for him to do exactly what he said he wanted to do.

****

"You all set, Turner?"

I peek my head into his office as he is just hanging up the phone. He sneaks a quick, guilty look my way as if I have caught him doing something wrong. And maybe I have.

Maybe he has secretly gotten himself hooked on watching porn, or maybe he was e-mailing his lover? Shit. All the layers of my skin want to crawl off of my body at the thought of not being enough for him.

"As ready as I'll ever be."

He stands up and shuts down his computer, then grabs his suit jacket off the back of his chair. He places his hand on the small of my back and guides me out of his office. You know the sparks and electric shocks that crawl up your body and seep into your pores when the man you love touches you? They're not there like they always have been. There's nothing, no sense of affection in the way he touches me. It's like he's a damn robot being programmed what to do and I don't like this strange alien feeling coming over me. In fact, I despise it.

Shutting off all of the lights except for the one in the reception waiting area, we pass the front desk where Mandy has already left for the day. Turner pulls his keys from his jacket pocket and locks up the door, and without another word he heads toward the car.

"So, tell me more about Nolan," Turner says as he turns the radio down, speeding up as we hit the highway.

"Like I told you on the phone, he's a mini Zack. You're going to love him, Turner," I gush.

"I know I will, and I can't wait to meet him."

Turner seems more relaxed and back to his old self as we draw closer to my brother's house. He's like Jekyll and Hyde. Hot and cold. I have no clue what will come out of his mouth next or how he will react.

My palms start to get sweaty as we turn into Zack and Krista's neighborhood and anxiety starts to set in as we pull into their drive, but the minute we put the car into park and I see my brother walk out with the baby cradled close to him, everything dissipates.

I climb out of my car and walk up the sidewalk with my arms outstretched indicating that he hand the baby over to me.

"Hey, I just got home and I don't want to give him up yet," Zack says teasingly.

"Too bad, let me have him," I demand.

Zack hands him over to me and all is forgotten for the time being as I stare at my handsome nephew.

"Look at him, Turner." I pivot around so he can see. "Isn't he just the cutest little thing?" I give Turner a fleeting look to see his reaction. He takes a quick perusal of the baby and simply nods.

"You can hold him when I'm done."

"Hell, no. I am not holding him. I'll probably drop him or something."

He holds his hands up in protest and I can imagine the shocked look on my face as well. My throat instantly becomes dry at his sudden outburst and lack of attention toward the baby. My brother must pick up on my tense anger as he takes a few steps in Turner's direction sticking his hand out for him to shake.

"Turner, man. How was your trip?" Zack asks as I walk up the few steps into their house.

I want my brother to see what he thinks and to act like nothing is wrong, so I leave them be to have guy talk. I shut the door and walk into their house being extra cautious with every step.

I am so engrossed in this bundle of joy in my arms. I can't help it; he is the most handsome and perfect baby I have ever seen.

"Hey, Krista. How you feeling?" I sit down by her on the couch.

"I am worn out, deadbeat tired. But boy is it worth it every time I look at my little man, here." She reaches up and rubs the top of his head.

"He has so much brown hair; it's crazy, isn't it?" I ask while examining his beautiful hair and his tiny little features.

"Let's just hope it stays that way and he doesn't lose it all. Not a fan of bald-headed men." We both burst out laughing at her words.

"I bet you had quite the homecoming last night when your man got home, huh?"

Krista nudges me in the shoulder jokingly. Krista and I have always been extremely close. She's more than my sister in law; she's one of my best friends. I know I can trust her with anything, but she just had a baby and I know she would worry herself sick about this.

"It was incredible. He's not leaving me again, I can tell you that much, but it was so worth it to see you born, wasn't it, little man?"

I turn myself away from Krista and coo at the baby so she doesn't see the concern written all over me. I have never been able to put on a poker face and hide how I truly feel. In less than twenty-four hours, these unknown emotions have become more like an obsession. If I hadn't called my brother earlier, he would have noticed right away and badgered the hell out of me until I caved and either started crying or losing my shit.

I contemplate how peaceful Nolan is lying sound asleep with not a care in the world as I cradle him in my arms. Babies give you a sense of peace, especially one as perfect as this one.

The guys walk in a few minutes later and I try to hand the baby over to Turner, but he won't hold him.

"Fine, then. I will keep him all to myself."

Zack picks up on the sudden tension radiating off of me, carefully bringing the baby up to rest his head on my shoulder as I pat his little bottom. My eyes dart over to him in hopes of some sort of sign from him to affirm my suspicions of Turner's erratic behavior.

Something isn't right at all; I can feel it. I know my brother too well. He is watching Turner like a hawk, with a gaze that could cut him into a million pieces. What the hell happened outside? My instincts turn out to be spot on when my brother starts asking Turner all kinds of questions, tension crackling in his voice.

Am I the only one picking up on it? Turner acts oblivious to the drilling. Out of blue, Zack starts bringing up things from our past, things that only the four of us would know about. I don't know if it's Turner's delayed reaction to a few of the questions or if my nerves are so frazzled from everything in my head, but the hairs on the back of my neck begin to rise. I need to get out of this room.

Neither one of them pay me the slightest bit of attention when I leave. I head into the baby's room and lay him down in his adorable crib, pulling his tiny comforter over him. He's so peaceful as I as I stand there watching him.

"He's something else isn't he?" Zack whispers from the doorway.

"He is. He's perfect, really."

I turn away from the crib and search my brother's face for any clue as to what he is thinking now. Zack's forehead is crinkled, worry sketched all over his face.

"What is it?" I ask softly, not wanting to wake the baby.

"Listen to me, I need to make this quick. Something is off about him; I knew it the minute he said he wouldn't hold Nolan."

I try to respond but Zack grips my hand, squeezing it gently as he places a finger over my mouth to shush me.

"Not a word. We will get through dinner and let me handle this. In the meantime, you have to continue to act as if you suspect nothing, Clove. Can you do that?"

I nod. More confusion and concern settles deep into my gut.

"I have one question."

Zack leans his head out the door then directs his attention right back to me.

"Go ahead."

"Should I be worried? I mean, what the hell is going on? You drilled him in there; it felt more like an inquisition."

Zack places his hands on my shoulders.

"Do you trust me, Clove?" he asks gravely.

"Of course I trust you. Why?"

"Then just do what I ask. Act like everything is normal and I promise you, I will find out what the hell is going on."

"Okay."

Zack must hear the worry in my voice as he brings me in for a tight hug, placing a kiss on my forehead. We're interrupted by Krista calling to us that dinner is ready. He releases me and as I follow him down the hall, I say a silent prayer for strength. Something tells me this is going to be a shock to my system that is going to slash my heart wide open, and all I can do is stand there and watch myself bleed.

****

Turner seems to be back to normal and talk comes rather easily to all of us during dinner. Zack puts up quite a front pretending everything is fine, until he notices the way Turner constantly sneaks glances at Krista. Every time she gets up, he checks her out from head to toe.

Krista is one of the most gorgeous women you will ever meet, both inside and out, with her long legs and long, wavy blonde hair. She has a face like a supermodel with small features and big, blue eyes. You can barely tell that she just had a baby. She gained only twenty-five pounds during her pregnancy and Nolan weighed a little over eight.

She's a complete knockout, but to have my husband eye-fucking her right in front of his wife, let alone her husband, is about as low as you can get. I could poke his damn eyeballs out with my fork. By the look on Zack's face, I can tell that thunder is brewing and lightning is striking in his head.

I don't have the slightest clue how to handle any of this or what in the fuck I am going to do. One thing I know for certain is that I'd better get Turner out of this house, because the way my brother's eyes are shooting daggers at him, it's not going to be long before he is up out of his chair and in Turner's face, and there will be nothing I can do to save him. Once you have pissed off Zack Becker, he'll massacre you with his bare hands.

I pick up my plate and help Krista clear the table. Normally, I would stay and help her clean up, but I think it's best to get Turner out of Zack's reach, now.

Krista seems surprised by our abrupt departure, but I can tell she's more tired than she lets on because she doesn't say a word about it. *I will call you tomorrow*, Zach mouths at me over her shoulder as I hug and kiss her goodbye.

Chapter Four

"Since when do we listen to head banging heavy metal?"

Reaching over and turning down the radio, I give my crazy ass husband a revolted look. Since saying our goodbyes to Zack and Krista, my husband has been acting normally, drawing slow circles with his hand on my leg . . . until he turned on the radio and found this music.

Now, he is pouring his heart and soul into doing his best to try and sing to whatever the song is playing on the radio. Not that I don't like this kind of music, but the entire car feels like it is shaking because he has it up so loud. My eardrums are about ready to fucking burst, not to mention I am so pissed off at him I can hardly hold this shit in anymore.

"What the hell is your problem, Clove? You have been acting like a complete and utter bitch today. If you have an issue with me then spit it the fuck out."

I don't even know how to respond to that rude remark. *I'm* acting strange? What the hell? Oh, how badly I want to reach across this console and shove those words right back down his throat and choke him with them.

"Well? Are you going to answer me or not?" he demands. I whip my head around and glare at him.

"You just called me a bitch, Turner, something you have never done before! You really want to know what my FUCKING problem is?" I lean over and get right in his face. "It's the fact that you were practically fucking Krista with your goddamned eyes right in front of me and Zack. *That's* what my fucking problem is!" I seethe.

"I did no such thing. Have you completely lost your mind?" The expression on his face looks as if I have just bitch slapped him.

"No, but I am beginning to think that you have lost yours." I poke my finger in his chest as I spit out my words.

"Damn, baby, I am sorry again. Why would I do something like that when I have you to look at all day long? When I was looking at her, all I was thinking about was how good she looked after just having a baby. Jesus Christ, Clove! I can't believe you would think that of me. That stings, here." He taps himself over his heart.

Fuck! This is so damn aggravating, this back and forth bullshit and keeping my inkling of Turner's infidelity, or whatever the hell kind of secret he is hiding, to myself. I take a deep breath then exhale slowly.

"You're right, and I am sorry, too. I just . . . I don't know what I am thinking. I don't have a problem with you, Turner. I really don't," I lie again, and thank God that it is dark out so he cannot see my face.

Fuck it. I don't want to argue with him anymore, I just want to distance myself from my emotions, climb into my bed, and wake up relieved that this was one big, ugly nightmare. *Yeah, right,* I chuckle to myself. How in the hell can I do that when the one who is holding my emotions in the palm of his hands is sitting right next to me? This sure as hell is no nightmare, this is a damn hurricane that has stormed into my life out of nowhere and laid at my damn doorstep filling my entire world with nothing but terror.

Silence fills the car the rest of the way home. I need the silence just as much as I need to sleep. I just can't seem to turn off my brain. The things Zack both did and didn't say have me on edge. I'm scared, worried, nervous, and above all, concerned about my brother's uncertainties regarding Turner.

If I don't start acting like myself then Turner is going to suspect I know something. He's not one to be easily manipulated. Maybe I should seduce him when we get home and remind him of everything that we've shared.

I take a glance at his handsome features in the dark out of my peripheral vision.

God, he is so achingly handsome with his manly, dark stubble. Who wouldn't want him any way they could have him? He has a gregarious personality and one hell of a stellar smile. A piece of art sculpted to perfection.

I am so in love with this man and my heart is broken and beating silently in my chest. I just cannot believe he would do this to me . . . to us. And why? Is it me? Am I not adventurous enough in bed with him? Am I not good enough for him anymore? They say your partner will stray elsewhere to get the sexual satisfaction they need. Have I pushed him away? Never, not once.

Our appetite for one another is way above average; I know this from talking to my girlfriends whenever we're together. None of their husbands seem to have either Turner's sex drive or his stamina. Hell, my friend Shelly says she gets more out of her BOB than she does her husband.

"At least my vibrator will do everything I ask him to," she always says.

But not Turner. I never have to ask him to do a thing; he just does it and does it well. *Stop!* I scream at myself. *You're driving yourself crazy.*

"Clove? We're home, babe."

My eyes pop open and I jump in my seat, noticing that we're in our garage.

"You dozed off for about ten minutes. Come on. Let's get inside and get ready for bed."

He reaches down and unhooks my seatbelt and then undoes his own. We both climb out of the car and head into the house, where I toss my purse and iPad onto the counter. I retrieve a bottle of water out of the fridge and make my way up the stairs without a backwards glance.

I am so exhausted right now that even the autopilot I have been running on for the past day and a half is burning out.

"I'm going to go take a nice, long bath before bed," I call out.

"Sounds good. I'll be up in a bit," he says casually.

I pour a small amount of lavender scented bath oil into the tub and adjust the water to as hot as I can possibly stand it. I look around and admire the beauty of this room, the one room I demanded we remodel when we bought this house three years ago.

It's exactly how I pictured it to be. Everything is white except the floor, which is a deep navy blue. The shower is off to the left and surrounded by glass with the same color blue tile covering one wall. That shower is Turner's favorite spot for us to make love. It was his only request when we remodeled, to have a walk in shower large enough for the two of us, while my request was this huge, round bathtub where we could both lie back and relax during the big tax season.

I sigh and brush away a lone tear at the thought of the many times we have made love in this bathroom. The morning he left, I was standing right in front of the double sink vanity applying my makeup when he crept up behind me, wrapping me in his big, strong arms. He started kissing the back of my neck all the way down my spine until he reached my ass, where he massaged my cheeks and slowly pulled my panties down my legs.

Without either one of us saying a word, he spun me around to face him and buried his face between my legs. It was mere seconds before I erupted all over him, and when he lifted me up on the counter, spread me wide, and slammed into me, the only sounds coming out of our mouths were our pants and moans. Our eyes locked on each other said everything.

He loves me, I have no doubt about it at all . . . and yet, why do I feel like the man downstairs is a stranger to me?

I strip out of my clothes then step in and submerge myself as deep as I can, trying to relax. It doesn't take long for the steam and the warmth from the tub to loosen me up.

Just as I am about to turn on the jets, the bathroom door opens and in walks Turner, completely naked.

My mouth goes dry as my gaze slides straight to his cock. It's thick and hard and pointing right at me. I lick my lips and suddenly, the familiar ache between my legs that only looking at my husband can bring on, is back. Even though a little voice in the back of my head wonders if his dick has been in anyone else lately, I still want him. He's MINE.

"Do you want to get in here with me?" I say invitingly.

"I don't want to get in the bathtub, Clove, but I sure as fuck want to get in you."

His eyes roam over every inch of my body and I want him inside me so badly. I would give anything to reconnect with my husband and make love to him, but by the way he is looking at me, making love is not what he has in mind. He wants to fuck my brains out. Well, if that is what Turner wants, I will do anything, and I mean anything, to save my marriage.

I eagerly arise from the tub and go to grab a towel, but he beats me to it. He bends down and starts lightly patting my skin with it to dry me off. Starting at my toes, he works his way up to my chest. Once he's standing, he drops the towel to the floor and caresses my smooth, oily skin.

"Your skin is so soft. It's flawless." I am mesmerized and can't even speak as he moves and cups my breast with his hands. "I don't want to fight with you anymore, Clove. I fucking hate it."

He drops his head and takes one nipple in his mouth, sucking hard. I let out a gasp and the deep breath that I didn't even know I was holding.

"I hate fighting with you too, lover boy," I moan.

Turner releases my nipple and moves over to the other, where he sucks even harder. He moves his other hand to cup one of the cheeks of my ass and pulls me into him.

"I've been a dick since I've come back, Clove," he says, releasing my nipple and bringing his head up to look me in the eye. "Forgive me."

"I forgive you," I smile.

"Good. Because I need to fuck you right here and right now."

I form my mouth into an O at his blunt words.

"What if I just want you to make slow, passionate love to me instead?" I ask, linking my hands together around his neck.

His facial expression changes from lust to confusion and his lips get tight as he draws them into a stiff line.

"If that's what you want?" he asks, his words strained.

I become more and more self-conscious as I stand there, watching him struggle with the concept of making love to his wife. Fuck, I know I should say something, but I reel my feelings in. I just don't know the right words to say. In the end I concede, and lift up on my tiptoes and bite gently on his bottom lip.

"All I want is you, babe."

Removing my hands from around his neck, I place them around his hard shaft and begin to stroke him. He hisses and lets out the loudest growl I have ever heard from him as I continue with one hand and graze my other over his balls, rolling them gently in my hand.

"Fuck, your hands are so smooth. I don't want gentle, Clove. I want it rough and I want it hard and I want it now, so get on your hands and knees."

He takes a step back and I lose my grip as my eyes become wide with shock. Doing what he says anyway, I kneel down on the soft white rug on the floor on all fours. I feel him position himself behind me, placing the tip of his dick just at the edge of my opening. He pulls it away and I whimper, making him chuckle.

"Are you craving me, Clove?" he asks, seizing my hair in his hands and yanking my head back. "Answer me, Clove. I said, are you craving me?"

"Y- yes. I'm craving you, Turner. I always crave you."

And then he is filling me completely. I scream at the top of my lungs at the way he brutally slams into me.

"Fuck." He stills himself inside me. "I love the way you clamp down on my cock the instant I'm inside you. Now, I do believe I said I wanted to fuck my wife, so hang on, baby girl."

And fuck me he does, his balls slapping mercilessly against my ass. He's fucking me hard as his entire upper body spoons my back. The grip he has on my sides is almost too painful, but I welcome it and I crave it and I want it.

"Holy fucking shit! Squeeze my dick, Clove. Squeeze every fucking drop of come out of my dick."

His words sound just as ruthless as his fucking is. Everything in my vision turns from white to black to red as he pounds over and over again, until I feel myself building up to explode. Finally, the muscles of my walls clench around him all on their own as my orgasm rips through me and I call out his name. He follows just a few seconds behind, stilling himself as he pours everything he's got into me. Our breathing still heavy, he releases his grip on my sides and I crumble to the floor with him on top of me.

"God, you're amazing. And you're all mine, Clove. All mine," he whispers, panting as we lay on the floor covered in sweat.

"I will always be yours, Turner. Always."

****

All morning long, I have been hiding my nerves by keeping myself busy. While the two of us were getting ready for work, I wandered around the house picking things up, doing this or that. Here at work I had a lot more to occupy my time, but now I'm sitting here at my desk willing my damn phone to ring with a call from Zack. I can't take any more of this waiting or I am going to drive myself even crazier than I already am.

"I'm calling him," I murmur.

I peek my head out the door, noticing Turner has the door to his office shut. Usually that indicates he does not want to be disturbed. Good, neither do I. I shut mine and lean my head back against it, taking a deep breath before I swipe the screen on my phone and hit call on Zack's name.

"Clove," he answers immediately.

"Hey. Sorry to call. I know it's still early, but please tell me you are working on things or you have found something out?" I run my hands through my hair with unsteady fingers.

"I'm working on it as we speak. I need a few days, sis. Can you give me that?"

"What choice do I have?"

I regret the words as soon as they spill out of my mouth. "I'm sorry Zack. I know you're trying to do everything you can to protect me. It's just, I don't know what to expect. He's different in so many ways. Ways I don't feel comfortable talking to you about."

"Has he hurt you?" he demands. I wince at his reaction.

"God, no. Not in the way you mean, at least. He may be breaking my heart right now, but he would never lay a hand on me. Ever."

The silence from the other end of the line doesn't sit well with me as I begin to pace the floor in front of my desk.

"Zack."

"I'm still here. You know you can talk to me about anything, right?"

"I know I can, Zack, and I love you for always being there for me. I- I'm just so fucking tense. This is my life we are talking about here."

My brother growls, barking out orders to someone about hurrying the hell up. I hope whatever he's yelling about has something to do with my situation.

"Clove, I really have to go. Give me till the end of the week to investigate all of this. I have a hunch and I am going with my gut. I know this is hard for you, I really do, and if you need me at all for anything, day or night, call me and I will be there."

My brother's attempts to try and soothe me set me a little at ease. Why do I feel like this is going to be the slowest week of my life?

****

God, I have never wanted a workweek to be over as bad as this one. It has been one thing after another. Clients demanding this or that, saying, 'No, that can't be right' when they look at their monthly financial reports. Every time it happens I have wanted to retort, 'Yes, it's right. Your business would have a ton more money if you didn't spend it on your personal shit.' Gah, drives me nuts! Thank goodness the weekend is finally here and the week from hell is over.

Turner has washed away all doubts in my mind about his infidelity. I finally got the nerve to ask him about the strange things I have noticed since his return. He explained about the cigar bar and how several of the guys went there one night after the conference. He says that he stayed for one drink and then left.

As we eased into our conversation, I quizzed him about his sexual behavior. He plunged into a long story about how several of the guys were talking about their sex lives. At first I was like, *what? Guys actually do that?* I thought only us girls talked about that kind of stuff.

"Did you tell them about ours?" I immediately asked.

"Hell, no," he said. "I don't want any other man having visions of my beautiful wife."

For my part, I made it clear that I loved sweet, kind, and even rough sex, as long as it was with him. I told him I would do anything he asked me to do if he wanted to try new things. He wasted no time listing all the things he wanted to do to me, and God, I just want to be done here and get started on all of them.

Last night was the best night's sleep I have had since he returned home. We made love slowly and it felt just as good as when he took me hard and fast. I should never have mistrusted him in the first place. Turner loves me, and for me to doubt that love is a feeling that I never want to experience again.

Zack and I have talked briefly a few times on the phone since that awful dinner. Even after I told him my insecurities were entirely erased, he still insisted on checking things out just to put his own mind at ease. I'm okay with that if it's going to make Zack happy and remove all his suspicions as well.

Both Turner and I have been cooped up in our offices all day every day, documenting financial transactions and summarizing several of our clients' financial statuses. I'm exhausted.

Turner being gone last week has put us behind with a few of our accounts. Now that the end of the week is here, I feel like I can breathe again as I e-mail the last of my reports to a client.

I look at the clock and realize I still have an hour left. Turner is on a conference call, therefore I can't ask him if he wants to skip out a little early and get to the bar for happy hour. Reaching for my phone, I decide to kick back and relax and maybe download some new songs. I plug in my phone to keep it charged and start listening to some music as I browse through the new selections.

"Clove?"

I jump, catching sight of Zack out of my peripheral vision.

"Christ, you scared the shit out of me!"

I sit back in my chair with a smile on my face, placing my hand over my heart as I slump back in my seat. I laugh, finding the situation funny. Pulling my ear buds out, I watch my brother as he strolls in and sits across from me at my desk. But he's not laughing or smiling.

"There's something wrong," I say in a strangled voice.

"Yeah, there is."

"Is . . .?"

I start crying and can't seem to get any words to come out. My chest starts heaving and I hold onto the edge of my desk, my knuckles snow white from my tight grip.

"Is he cheating on me?"

"It's worse, Clove. Much worse."

The way he looks at me tells me whatever his news is, it's going to rip me to shreds.

"Wha-what is it?" I can barely choke the words out.

"Remember the bachelor and bachelorette parties we threw for you and Turner when you got married?"

"Yeah." My eyebrows knit together. Where is he going with this?

"You remember how all of us guys went to a bar and a chick tried hitting on Turner? He got up to go to the bathroom and the chick followed him in, but the chick wasn't really a chick?"

"Yeah, I remember."

"Well, it seems Turner doesn't. When I was talking with him and joking with him about it, he said something that didn't make any sense. He said, 'that chick was hot. I'd never cheat on your sister, but if I were single I definitely would've done her.' "

"What?"

"Exactly. How would he forget something like that? It's not possible."

Neither of us says anything for a few drawn-out seconds.

"I am confused, Zack. Where are you going with all of this?"

"I ran his prints, Clove."

"You . . . you ran his finger prints? But why?"

Zack leans in and the look he gives me has me suddenly standing up from out of my chair.

"I suspected something wasn't right from that moment on, Clove. That's why I ran his prints. There is no way in hell he wouldn't have remembered that she wasn't a chick."

We stare at each other for an eternity as I grasp the implications all at once. Zack's face drops and he is up out of his seat in no time at all, catching me as my legs give out beneath me.

"Jesus Christ, no!" I wail, shaking my head back and forth.

"He's not your husband, Clove. The man you brought home from the airport is Turner's identical twin brother, Trent Calloway."

"What the hell are you talking about, Zack? Turner doesn't *have* a twin brother. He doesn't have any siblings at all!"

"I hate to tell you this, Clove, but it's true. We were able to track down a birth certificate for this fucker with the information we had. He is definitely Turner's twin."

"But . . . why didn't he ever tell me? He's never mentioned, not once, that he had a brother, much less an identical twin! And his mother! In all this time she has never talked about another son or even said she has had other children. I- I don't understand this at all. Turner has never lied to me before, ever."

How many more secrets and lies are waiting to be uncovered in this whole mess? It was bad enough when I thought my husband was cheating on me, but this? Then, like a ton of fucking bricks, it finally hits me that the man I have been sleeping with for the last week is not my husband, but his brother. *His identical twin brother*. I feel sick as my stomach starts twisting and churning.

"W- Where's Turner?" I whisper in horror.

"I have no fucking idea at this point, Clove, but I am sure as hell going to find out. Who the fuck is this guy and what does he want?"

His face turns stoic and I can't breathe with all of this shit running through my head.

"Oh, my God. Zack. Where in the hell is my husband? We have to find him!"

"Clove." Zack shakes me, gripping my shoulder tightly. "Listen to me, Clove."

He gently coaxes me back down in my chair.

"Look, I cannot imagine how you're feeling right now, but you need to pull yourself together and listen to me. Can you do that?"

I can't even answer him. My body goes into full force shock. I feel myself trembling as the room spins around me.

"What the hell am I going to do, Zack?"

My lips begin to quiver and tears start to slip down my cheeks. The look on my brother's face is full of pain and anger.

"You've got to help me find my husband, Zack."

"We're going to find him, sis," he says, kneeling down next to me. "But I can't do this without your help."

"My help? What do you need me to do?"

"Damn it!"

He gets up and starts pacing the floor.

"It's going to kill you to do this, Clove, but you have to leave him. There is no way in hell I am allowing you to stay with some psychopath. I want you the hell out of there, NOW." His entire body shakes as he pleads with me. "I don't have any more answers right now."

My body has gone into a complete state of denial. How could this be happening to Turner and me? Our lives were perfect.

"I should have gone with him like he wanted me to," I sob, nearly losing my ability to speak, straining to even get those few words out as a lump too hard to swallow forms in my throat.

"No. Don't say that. This is not your fault, you hear me? Something tells me this would have happened one way or another, Clove, and until we find some answers, I need to know you're safe. The safest place for you to be right now is at my house."

The expression on my brother's face is killing me. He's worried and hurting as badly as I am. And now I am about to hurt him even more.

"Do you know exactly what this means, Zack? If I leave him not knowing where Turner is, will he kill him when I'm gone? I can't do it. I refuse to leave and walk around wondering what might happen," I say adamantly through the tears streaming down my face . . . tears for Turner, tears for my brother, tears for myself.

"I don't know if I can handle you being there, Clove. You know nothing about him or his motives. Do I have to beg you to get you to do it?"

"You can beg all you want, I won't, and I can't do it. I love Turner too much to not try and help find him. You have to understand that Zack, please don't fight me on this."

I wring my hands in my lap, silently begging my brother to let me stay and figure out why Trent Calloway has taken over my husband's life.

"Fucking hell, Clove!" Zack hisses, running his hands through his hair before looking me right in the eyes.

"Fine. As much as I hate the idea, if you can muster up enough strength to help do this job, it might be our only chance to find out where Turner is. Are you prepared to act as if you know absolutely nothing? And the idea of him even touching . . . *Son of a bitch!* I can't even get my mind to go there. You're my sister, Clove. My job as your brother is to protect you, keep you safe. I can't do that while you're living in your house with that cocksucker. Do you know how hard it is for me not to grab that fucking piece of shit by his balls right now and drag his ass off to jail so I can beat the fuck out of him until he tells me where Turner is? Do you?" he shouts.

"Zack, I can only imagine how hard this is for you. I need you to imagine how hard it is for me and to put yourself in my shoes."

He throws me a dark look as he continues raking his hands through his hair.

"I'll do whatever it takes to get Turner back, no matter what it is I have to do," I say defiantly.

Even if that means beating Trent Calloway at his own game.

Chapter Five

Exactly how the hell I am going to act like I don't want to slice this piece of shit's throat the minute he is ready to leave is beyond me. Zack and I didn't really have much time to talk or strategize any of this out before he had to leave; I have so many questions running through my mind.

"God, Turner, where are you?" I whisper.

Turner was an only child, for God's sake. How could this be? His father took off when he was two and neither his mom nor Turner ever heard from him again. It was as if he fell off the face of the earth. And Melody, his mom, has kept the fact that he has an identical twin brother a secret. How could she do that? The biggest question is, *why* would she do that? And what does Trent expect to gain from stealing his brother's identity?

The thing that is tearing me up more than anything is the fact that I've had sex with him. No wonder he seemed so different. I've slept with another man a man who I don't even know and now that I know the truth about him, I have to pretend that I don't? I lay my head on my desk and I can't help but let the tears fall. My body is wracked with deep, body-thrashing sobs. Tears continue to fall as my heart feels the pain and torment of what is happening all around me. I need Turner, *my* Turner.

"Oh, God!" I scream.

"Clove! What in the hell is the matter, sweetheart?"

That voice. The voice sounding just like my Turner is asking me if I am all right? Fucking hell no! I am not all right, you asshole. You have destroyed my life, so fuck no, I am NOT ALL RIGHT.

I can't look up at him yet. Keeping these murderous thoughts to myself, I shake my head back and forth in pure disgust at myself for what I have done and what I will have to do.

I feel him place his hand on my back and I stiffen from his touch. Pull yourself together, Clove and think. Think! I lift my tear stricken face off of my desk.

"I have a horrible headache," I mumble and try to gauge his reaction to see if he knows that at times I come down with migraines.

"Is it another one of your migraines?" He asks with his fake concern.

Oh, this asshole is good. How he knows about my headaches makes me wonder what else he knows about me. He knows everything. I just know he does.

"I think so. Do you mind if we skip out on our plans for tonight? I just want to go home and take a pill and climb into bed."

"No, not at all. Let's get you home. You know I hate it when my girl doesn't feel well."

Oh, how I want to slap him across his smug face as he removes his hand from my back, then strides to the table on the other side of the room to bring me back a box of Kleenex. With shaky hands I remove a few and wipe my face, stand, and gather my belongings without a thank you or another word to him.

Now that I know the truth about this man not being my husband, the thought of being anywhere near him repulses me. Until I can come to grips with all of this I need to stay as far away from him as possible. I need time to think and time to plan how the hell I am going to deal with the fact that the man I am sharing a bed with is not the man that I love.

I should win a damn award for best actress as we drive home and I am forced to listen to this stranger who looks just like my husband ramble on about how he is going to take care of me when we get home. I don't want him to take care of me. I want my *husband* to take care of me!

As Trent soothingly runs his hands through my hair as we drive home, I take the time to study him in profile. Everything about him looks so similar to Turner's distinctive features . . . eye color, hair color, body size, even the shape of his head. Their voices are the same, too. My head really does start to ache as I think about the one thing that truly sets them apart from one another- it's the way they have sex. Turner is so gentle and kind and worships every part of my body and Trent fucks. Plain and simple, he just fucks. I recoil as far into my seat as I can, shying away from his touch and laying my head against the window.

"Almost home. Do you need me to stop and get you anything?"

Every time I hear that voice it takes me further into a state of heartbreak.

"No. Just get me home. Sorry about ruining our plans for tonight."

I remain still with my eyes closed.

"Hey, don't be sorry. I hate seeing you like this. You're the most important person in the world to me, Clove, and you know it."

No, asshole, I don't know it. Whatever your reason is for doing this, it seems to me you're the most important person in your world, you bastard. God, I wish I could tell him how I feel.

"It will be good to just sit around and do nothing. It's been one hell of a week at work."

His voice sounds a little irritable.

An epiphany hits me when he mentions work. How in the hell has he pulled off pretending to be Turner for almost a week now, even at the office? Has he been stalking us and watching our every move? How did he know where we lived after I picked him up from the airport? And my home! He knows where everything is. He walked right in the other day and he knew.

Jesus Christ, he knows my morning routine. He knows almost everything about me. How does he know all this?

Unless . . . oh God, no. He's been in our home when we haven't been there. He might even have hidden cameras all over the house, seeing as how he's so familiar with the most private details of my life.

All of a sudden I am fuming. I want to claw his eyes out and scream at him, to demand for him to tell me where Turner is. Why? What in the hell could my husband have possibly done to him to make this crazy fucker want to destroy him? But I can't. I sure as hell know who can, though, and after my brother and I figure out exactly what it is that we need to do, the first person I am going to pay a not-so-friendly visit to will be Melody.

"What can I do to make you feel better?" the sick bastard asks as we enter my house. My damned house, not his. Mine and Turner's.

Get the fuck out of here and go get my husband, you sick and twisted fucker, is what I really want to say. Turner would never ask me, 'what can I do?' He would just do it because he knows me.

"Nothing," is what actually comes out. I toss my purse on the counter as I normally do and set off towards the stairs. "I am just going to take a pill and climb into bed."

"Clove." His voice startles me as I begin to ascend. "Wait a second, Clove."

He wraps his arms around me from behind. Thank God he cannot see my face because I feel tears starting to well up in my eyes again.

"I'll be right down here if you need anything, so just holler, okay?"

He kisses the top of my head and squeezes me just a little tighter before releasing me.

I really have to get my act together or he is going to catch on to the fact that I know he is an impostor. I continue up the stairs and enter my bedroom, softly closing the door. A calmness settles in my heart when I notice my wedding picture sitting on the dresser.

I draw nearer and run my hands over Turner's face. Tears of both outrage and pain relentlessly fall as I look down at him, blurring my vision. Covering my mouth for fear that Trent will hear me, I just stand there and stare at the man I love, wondering what he must be feeling right now. If he knows what is going on, he must be as scared to death for me as I am for him.

"I am so in love with you, Turner Calloway," I whisper.

I scrutinize the picture that was taken on the best day of my life and study the features I know so well. It's remarkable how identical the two of them truly do look. The more I stare, the angrier I become, and the more determined I am to get to the bottom of this nightmare.

Pulling my glance away from the picture, my gaze drifts over to Turner's closet. With slow steps I enter and I am surrounded by the strong smell of my man.

I fumble my way through all of his clothes, desperate to find the shirt I am looking for. I toss clothes all over the floor until I find the dark blue shirt that we bought for him on our honeymoon. I bring the shirt up to my nose and sniff, triggering my tears again. I slip down to my knees, crying and rocking myself back and forth on his closet floor.

I have never been so scared of anything in all of my life. I need him, and he needs me. We belong together. There is no fucking way I am going to let anyone take him away from me. Sitting on my knees for God knows how long surrounded by all things Turner, I vow to him and to myself that I will find him and bring him home where he belongs.

Even though it's the beginning of summer and warm outside, I remove my clothes and change into a pair of sweats and Turner's t-shirt. Right now the thought of my skin touching *his* makes my body shudder. I feel as if I am going to suffocate. The information I need to find Turner lies within the man downstairs; it's only a matter of time before he is going to want to touch me again and I am going to have to let him. If I don't, I may never see my husband again.

Can I do this now that I know the truth? I thought my husband was having an affair; never in my wildest dreams could I ever have imagined the real reason he was acting so differently. More guilt and shame eat away at me for doubting my Turner at all.

I feel somehow disconnected from my mind, body, and soul as I try and separate my old reality from the nightmare happening all around me. Turner is everywhere in this house, in our bedroom, and in this bed. This bed where I have slept with another man. How long am I going to be stuck in this never-ending cycle of deceit?

Curling myself up in a ball, I lay there in the dark and wonder where my husband is. Is he safe? Alive? He has to be alive. I close my eyes and picture my brave man and pray that wherever he is, he knows how much I love him and that everything I have to do is because he's everything to me.

I believe in soul mates, and Turner is and always will be mine, even if this destroys us. But then I realize that it doesn't matter what I say or do, now. I am never going to be able to forgive myself, and Turner is never going to look at me the same way again. He is never going to want me, knowing someone else has had me. Our lives are ruined, and for what?

Even though my back is to the bedroom door, I feel Trent standing in the doorway. Staying as still as possible so that he thinks I am sleeping, I lay there and wait for him to climb into bed. When he does, I still don't move.

Please don't touch me. Not yet.

But he does. He moves closer to me and wraps his arms around me, tucking himself in close. I don't want to acknowledge his presence but I can't risk tipping him off.

"Hey," I murmur.

"Hey, sweetheart. You feeling better?" he says softly.

"Not really."

And it's the truth.

"I'm sorry. I wish I knew what to do to make you feel better."

"You know the only thing that makes me feel better when I get these headaches is sleep, Turner," I sigh.

He lets out a frustrated breath and loosens his hold from around my waist. I can smell the alcohol on his breath and with his arms around me and that smell, my gut starts churning and I feel like I could be sick.

Pushing all those thoughts back and curling into his touch, I close my eyes knowing that I won't feel better until I have my husband's arms around me, not the arms of a stranger. A stranger who scares me, a man I have a feeling will kill my husband and me if he ever finds out what I know.

Chapter Six

There's a strange feeling of weight on my chest when I wake up. Some is from the arm draped across me, pinning me to Trent's side. The biggest weight comes from that of regret, hurt, anger, and sadness.

It's Saturday, and knowing I have to spend the next two days alone with this man repulses me. Needing to get up and use the bathroom, I gently lift his arm off of me. I don't really want to wake him; he may want me to come back to bed with him and I am just not ready to play the part of his doting wife yet.

Tiptoeing into the bathroom and locking the door, I turn on the shower as hot as I can. After using the toilet I shimmy out of my clothes, and as I lift the shirt over my head and it glides over my face, I am assaulted with the smell of Turner. His fresh, clean sent reminds me of what lies ahead.

I inhale deeply one last time before I pull it the rest of the way over my head and drop it to the floor. I step under the hot spray; picking up the soap, I scrub my body from head to toe trying to erase the smell of the sick asshole who is lying in my bed.

I don't even realize how hard I am actually scrubbing until a sharp sting on my arm causes me to look down and notice that my arm is turning the brightest shade of red. I immediately stop, letting the soap slip out of my grasp.

I place my hands over my face as I lean my head back, turning my attention to my hair. I give it the same treatment, using more shampoo than necessary and washing, rinsing, and repeating three damn times. I turn and let the hot spray pound on my chest as if to wash away all the pain of my bleeding and tortured heart.

The minute I step out of the shower and start to dry myself off, though, I realize that I forgot to grab clothes to put on. I curse under my breath.

Having to walk into the bedroom to collect my clothes means having to walk out with just my towel wrapped around me. I stand and stare at the handle of the door for several minutes and hope like hell that Trent is still sleeping. I can do this. I have to do this- there isn't any other way around it.

Opening the door as quietly as I can and not looking at the bed, I tiptoe over to my closet and grab the first pair of shorts and shirt that I can find. Making my way over to my dresser, I do the same thing with my bra and panties.

"If I could wake up every morning and see my beautiful wife standing there looking sexy as hell, I would be one hell of a lucky man."

I flinch as I look over my shoulder and see Trent lying down with his hands behind his head and an 'I want to fuck you' look on his face.

"Sorry if I woke you."

Abruptly he is off the bed and standing directly in from of me.

"You didn't. Is your headache gone?"

His tone is caring, which I know is all a damn lie.

"It is," I lie too.

"Good, because I missed you last night." Bringing his mouth down, he kisses right above the top of my towel where it's wrapped tightly over my breasts. "Next time wake me up so we can shower together."

Not on your motherfucking life will I wake you up and let you EVER touch me in that shower. He lifts his head and runs his hands down my arms, causing chills of horror to ripple all over my body.

"I would love that." I smile and lean in to give him a soft peck on his lips. "What do you have planned today?" I ask as I turn from him and enter the bathroom, shedding the towel in record time and quickly getting dressed.

"Not quite sure. You?" he asks through the closed door.

"Krista called me yesterday and wants to meet for coffee. She's been dying to have some now that Nolan is here. Would you like to come with?"

Please say no.

"Nah, I'm good. I do want to go out tonight, though."

I grab my brush and pull it through my wet hair and gather it up in a ponytail.

"Sure. Do you want to go to the club like we planned last night?" I ask, turning and walking back into the bedroom. I pray like hell he is dressed.

"Let's do that," I hear him call out from the closet.

I let out the breath I was holding, which damn near made me pass out, and start to make the bed. I want to keep my daily morning routine the same so as not to throw him off. He reappears out of the closet fully dressed in my husband's clothes.

"What time will you be back?"

My anger climbs out of control as I see him standing there as if he owns the place. Keeping my murderous thoughts to myself, I rein in my anger and replace it with a bogus smile.

"Not too long." I go back to finishing up making the bed. "I do need to stop at the grocery store, though. Is there anything you would like me to pick up?"

He grins and stealthily makes his way over to me, putting his arms around me and guiding me slowly down onto my perfectly made bed.

"Just bring yourself back," he whispers hoarsely.

Within seconds his mouth is on mine. Even though the sight of him lying on top of me is nauseating, I submit to his kiss, lightly stroking my tongue against his. With persistent urgency, he plunges his tongue into my mouth and doesn't miss a beat as he swirls his tongue forcefully against mine.

Now that I know who this man really is, he definitely kisses so much differently than Turner. Turner's kisses are sweet and comforting and Trent's are demanding and full of temptation. A temptation that I am finding myself eagerly surrendering to.

My mind is telling me that it is wrong, oh so wrong, to enjoy the way he is kissing me, but my body has a mind of its own and at this very moment it's winning as I feel his steely erection press into my core. I'm weak and I need to stop, and yet somehow I can't. I clutch desperately at him, drawing him as close to me as I can.

I hate you. I hate you, I repeat over and over in my head.

"Holy shit, baby. If we don't stop now, you will never make it over to Krista's."

His voice is raspy and full of desire as he mouths his words against my lips. I blink several times as I realize what I have just done.

"You're right." Bracing my hands on his chest to gently coax him off of me. "I'll call you when I leave the store."

He takes my hands and pulls me up off the bed.

"Sounds good. Tell everyone I'll be over soon."

Lifting my phone off the dresser, I kiss him one last time on the cheek and with shaky legs, I descend the stairs in a blurry haze. I manage to grab my purse and make it out to my car before losing myself in a fit of tears. A lump forms in my throat as I pull out of my driveway. I slam my hands against the steering wheel as I speed down the road toward the coffee shop as all the guilt pours out of me at once and my heart sags into an empty pit of darkness.

****

I survey the parking lot of the coffee shop for Zack's truck. This is where we've decided to meet to try and come up with a plan, since we didn't have much time to figure things out when he broke this news to me yesterday. I will never forget the look of pain on my brother's face when he told me. Not seeing his truck anywhere in sight, I pull down my visor and look into the mirror.

"Jesus Christ, Clove. You're a fucking mess."

Reaching over and opening the glove box, I yank out a handful of Kleenex and wipe my eyes, trying to clean up my face as best as I can before my brother gets here and sees what a mess I am.

Oh, who am I trying to kid? I toss the dirty Kleenex onto the floor. He's my brother, for God's sake. He knows how much I love Turner, so he knows I am going to be a mess. As if on cue he pulls in right next to me, dashing out of his truck and whipping my car door open.

"Fuck. Clove. Come here."

He helps me get out of the car and I am engulfed in the best brotherly hug that I have ever had, one that is so very much needed.

"Shh. Come on. Let's get in the truck."

Zack extracts himself from my clingy body and opens his truck door for me to climb in. After shutting the door, he dashes to his side and steps up.

"Here," he says, handing me some Kleenex. "I can't imagine what you must be going through, Clove. It's okay to let out how you feel. I can't tell you what you need to do at home, sis, but I can tell you that I am doing everything humanly possible to try and find Turner. I need you away from that sick fuck like yesterday."

He places his hand on my shoulder and gives me a light squeeze. I know he still wants me to leave. I just can't. I have come to terms with the fact I have to stay; it's just a lot harder than I imagined.

"Does everyone at the station know about this?"

I turn my head and look out the window. I can't bear to look at my brother right now. I feel so deceitful. If I make it through this without killing either Trent or myself it will be a damn miracle. The guilt is eating me alive that in spite of knowing right from wrong, I still let myself succumb to Trent this morning.

"Martinez and the chief know, Clove. There are a few others as well, others that work for us. We're having Trent followed. We know his every move outside of the house. But . . ." He pauses and my head snaps around to look at him.

"But what?" My voice cracks. His empathetic look is confirmation of what I am dreading the most.

"You have to play your part in this, Clove. You have to be his wife."

"I- I don't know how to do that, Zack."

God, it's so hard talking to my brother about this. Zack places his hand over the top of mine.

"Look. I know how much you love Turner and want him home safe. That love is all you're going to need to get yourself through this."

My tears have turned into uncontrollable sobs now. I want my husband home and safe, and to feel his arms wrapped tightly around me. I am so ashamed of myself for the way I acted this morning when Trent kissed me. There is no way in hell I can tell my brother that, though. He'll think poorly of me. I start shaking.

"Clove, what is it?"

"Oh my God, Zack. Do you know what it's going to do to Turner when he finds out that I've slept with another man? This is going to destroy my marriage. He is so proud of the fact that he was my one and only. What if he can't get past that?"

I'm so frightened. And I don't like the look that my brother is giving me, either. I don't want his pity.

"Turner is a smart man, and he loves you just as much as you love him. I won't lie to you and say that any of this is going to be easy, because it's not. But Clove, you have to try and put all of that aside and focus on just being the sweet, loving wife you have always been. Something tells me this guy has done his homework and knows more about you and your daily routines than we think. The smallest thing could set him off."

"You're not telling me anything I don't already know, but Zack, I'm frightened."

"I know you are, Clove, but you're so strong and brave, and I will always be there for you. If at any time you feel threatened, you call me and I will be there to put his ass behind bars where he belongs."

"You can't arrest him or we will never find Turner!"

"Turner would put your life before his own, Clove. You know he would want you safe."

Hearing those words suddenly gives me strength. I know I will need a lot more of it by the time I get back home. Somehow, some way, I have to try and push all of this to the back of my mind.

"I don't want to talk about me anymore. I want to talk about how you're going to find Turner and bring him home."

He turns away from me as if he can't bear to look me in the eyes.

"We have a private investigator at the hotel where he was staying."

"Zack," I say apprehensively.

Sighing, he finally looks back at me.

"Look, Clove. I am not going to lie to you about this. It's going to be very hard to find him for the simple reason that those two look so much alike, and between the time that Turner left here and the time that he returned, we have no clue when he was abducted."

I feel like someone is stabbing me repeatedly with needles in my chest as I start to hyperventilate. It's suddenly too warm in my brother's air-conditioned truck. I suck in air as I try to breathe. Opening the door and climbing out, I bend over and try to catch my breath as my mind goes in a tortuous scramble of visions of my husband being bound and gagged and beaten, or worse, lying dead somewhere and never to be found.

"Breathe, Clove," Zack says soothingly in my ear.

"I- I don't know what to do Zack! I'm just so scared."

"I know you are. Come here, sis."

I stand up and my brother puts his arms around me.

"There is one more thing I need to tell you and then you have got to dig deep inside and pull all of your love for Turner to the surface. Can you do that?" he implores.

"I have to," I whimper. "I just don't know how."

"Love. Love for Turner will show you how."

And hearing the word 'love,' it feels like I can hear Turner's soothing voice calling out to me. I straighten my spine and dry my tears with the back of my hand as I listen to my brother tell me the plan that he has to find Turner. For the first time in more than twenty-four hours, I manage a smile. It's a small one, but then again I haven't smiled at any time whatsoever in days.

"I had to tell Krista about this. I hope you don't mind?" Zack tells me after we dump our empty coffee cups in the garbage on our way out the door from the coffee shop.

"Not at all. I suspected you would. I just don't want her worrying so much after just having a baby. It's bad enough that you have to be dragged away from the two of them like this."

"I'm only going to be gone for the day while I drive over to Turner's mother's house. I don't want you worrying about Krista or me. If anything at all happens while I am gone, you pick up the phone and call Martinez, you hear me?" he says sternly.

"I will," I reply back meekly.

Zack kisses the top of my head. I climb into my car and pull out with him directly behind me. I take a deep breath and let it back out as I head to the store, praying that the information we are so desperately looking for begins with Melody's answer as to why in the hell she has kept Trent's existence a secret for all of these years.

Chapter Seven

I've managed to get through the grocery store without breaking down or running into anyone I know. I remember to call Trent to let him know I am on my way home and even muddle through a big fat lie by telling him I would prefer to stay home and watch movies and just chill after our hectic workweek. There is no way I am prepared to face anyone in a public setting with him. I just don't have the confidence in myself to do it.

"Shit!" I scream in my car as I am driving down the road toward my house.

God, how could you be so dumb, Clove? I need to outsmart him and act like nothing is wrong. Turner and I have never stayed in two nights in a row, especially on the weekend, and if he's been studying us as closely as I think, he knows that. He has to. No, I am just going to say I missed being with him last night. He's a schemer and a very good liar . . . I just have to remind myself of this and play his game. I can do this. Well, me and the bottles of wine I bought can do this.

I reach across into the passenger seat and pat the bag holding the wine. Smart thinking, buying three bottles of my favorite wine. I hope like hell I get drunk and pass out in order to avoid any type of sexual activities taking place with him. I know that it has to happen sooner or later; it's just that I am choosing later. At least for tonight.

My palms are sweaty and my entire body is in turmoil as I pull into the drive and hit the button for the garage door. When I see Trent step out the back door and into the garage, I swallow the knot in my throat and pretend that it's Turner coming toward me. Love. That's what I keep telling myself as I step out of my car and he brings me into his arms.

"I missed you and I'm starving."

He presses himself into me.

"Starving for what?" Bile rises up from my stomach as he presses his hard erection firmly against my stomach.

"Starving for you," he replies in a sex-tinged voice.

"Oh."

Before I can say anything further, he backs me up against the car, pinning me with his rock solid body.

"When was the last time I told you that you have the most beautiful eyes?" He leans in and kisses right beside my left eye gently. "The perfect nose?" He kisses the tip of my nose. "A mouth that was made for kissing?" He nips at my bottom lip. "And tits that were made for sucking?"

He bends down and bites my nipple through my shirt.

"A pussy that is so tight and hot and fits my cock just perfectly?" he finishes, reaching down and cupping my core through my shorts.

He sounds just like Turner when he talks that way. For a brief moment I can pretend it really is him, but when I look deep into his eyes as he brings them to mine, the illusion is shattered. Those are not Turner's eyes staring back at me; those eyes are of a man who is possessed by some unknown demon, eyes that are eating me alive as he gazes into mine.

He must have been snooping while I was gone and read the birthday card that Turner gave me last year saying those exact same words. Knowing he is waiting for an answer, I tell him the truth as I skate my arms up his torso and clasp them behind his neck.

"Last year for my birthday, I do believe."

I focus on his lips instead of looking him in the eye. I am so petrified right now that my insides are shaking. I just want to scream for him to get off of me, but I can't.

"I am going to put these groceries away. You go upstairs and get naked and wait on our bed for me, because I have been dying to fuck you deep, hard, and fast ever since you walked out that door this morning."

Oh shit, oh no. I'm not ready for this. But I pull up on my tiptoes and bite hard on his bottom lip as if to tell him I can't wait. Ducking underneath his strong arms and making my way into the house, I run for the stairs only stopping when I reach my bedroom, and stare at my bed.

I pace back and forth, chewing my fingernails nervously. I feel weak and helpless but I have to persevere. I have no sense of direction here. What the hell am I going to do? I am so weak. Why? Why is this happening? I do not want to give myself to him. I'm in hell, absolute fucking hell, and I have no way of getting back to my piece of heaven.

I take a deep breath and slowly pull my shirt over my head, tossing it on the leather chair in the corner, then reach behind me and unclasp my bra slowly, dragging it down my arms as if I am stilling time. Tossing that along with my shorts and panties, I place one leg and then the other onto the bed. Before I can even turn myself around, I hear a low growl coming from the doorway.

"Stop right there, Clove."

Shit. I am naked and on all fours with my ass in the air. Take a deep breath, Clove. Love, remember?

I hear the hissing sound of a zipper then the soft thud of his jeans hitting the floor. Drawing in a long breath to calm my shaky nerves, I turn my head slightly to see him standing there naked and stroking his cock. I am so fucked and I do not mean in a good way either. I just can't seem to pull my eyes away from him. For some unknown reason it is turning me on watching him stroke himself with fire in his eyes as he watches me watch him. He's telling me that he likes it, too. I don't want to like it. I want to hate it as much as I hate him.

"I love your voluptuous ass. So round and tight and so damn perfect."

Keeping his hand on his dick, he stalks over to the edge of the bed. I tilt my head forward and close my eyes as I feel his hands start to touch and caress my legs. They make their way up until he is cupping handfuls of my bottom. I can't stand to look at him and I can't stand myself right now as he digs deeper with his fingers until both of his hands are sliding up and down and along the crack of my ass. Then, he stops. I feel the bed dip and his hands move down until one finger is sliding through my folds.

"Spread for me, baby. Let me feel that sweet, tight, hot pussy of yours."

And I do. I spread my legs as far as I can and lay my head against the silky comforter.

"Jesus Christ. Your fucking pussy is perfect," he growls.

His finger makes its way to my clit, where it presses firmly. I buck. It's as if he has pushed the 'on' button as he plays with it, swirling his finger around and pressing in at the same time. I'm panting hard as he spreads my folds with his other hand. His movements on my clit are repetitious and my body is blazing from his expertise.

The fucker is good at this, and he knows it. I'm just as sick and twisted as he is by enjoying and wanting more of what he is doing to my body. He's driving me crazy with desire. I hate my body for betraying my mind. I deserve to live in hell, but fuck me if this doesn't feel so damn good.

He removes his finger from my clit and I whimper as he chuckles behind me. He replaces it with his thumb and slides two fingers inside of me, curling them upward. I scream as he finds my sweet spot and applies soft pressure as he begins to move them in and out of me.

"You like that, baby?" he whispers at the base of my ear.

I had gotten so lost in his touch that I never realized his face was this close to mine. I feel him now as he lies gently on top of me. He stops his amazing yet torturous fingering.

"Do you want me to continue, Clove?" he asks, his voice dripping with cruelty.

"Yes, Turner," I plead.

At that, he pushes his fingers back in, continuing his carnal assault.

"FUCK!" I roar.

I throw my head back as his fingers work at an agonizingly fiery pace. He knows exactly what to do with those hands of his, and he's flawless with them.

His breathing is just as fast as mine is. I am losing my fucking mind and my will not to give this man my orgasm. But I can't, he's just too good. Somehow, he is a master at setting my body on fire.

Oh, how I don't want to give him this! It's killing me to not let go, but the brutal yet first-class finger fucking that he is giving me has me choking back sobs of unwanted ecstasy. In the end I give up, letting out an ear-piercing scream as I climax uncontrollably.

Before I can even recover, he is positioned behind me. I can't help myself now; I want him to fill me with his dick so desperately. I am digging and clawing at the comforter, physically aching with how badly I need him to fuck me. I am hungry for more of him and my heart races faster than it ever has as I press my ass into his cock.

"Fuck me now, Turner!" I demand. "Damn it . . . you better fuck me hard like you said you would."

And then it happens. He slams his glorious cock into my already drenched pussy.

He eases himself back out so just the head of his dick stretches my opening. God, does it feel so good. This man knows exactly what he is doing and he knows he does it well. He leans down and puts his weight on my back and I love it.

"You," he says. "I am going to fuck you and bring you so much sexual pleasure. You just stay on all fours with that sexy as hell ass in the air and let me take care of business back here."

His voice is rough and full of promise. My legs quiver as he removes his mouth from my ear. A loud hiss escapes his lips as he plunges into me again. I scream and throw my head back.

"Fucking hell, Clove. Tight, wet, and fucking warm. You ready, baby? Hold the hell on because you're about to get fucked raw."

The penetration is deep and delicious and I cannot get enough of him screwing me this way, hitting me deep and hard as his hands grab handfuls of my ass. Extending my right hand a little higher on the bed to help hold myself up, I take my left hand and slide it onto my clit and squeeze the folds of skin between my fingers, moving my hand from side to side and up and down.

"That's it, Clove. Touch it and make yourself come nice and hard all over my cock." His sultry voice echoes around the room. "You like being fucked, don't you Clove? You can't get enough of it, can you?"

His grunts and groans tell me he is loving what he is doing, too, as he thrusts in and out. I have never been fucked like this before, ever. My orgasm starts to build and I know when it hits, it's going to hit so hard that I am going to scream like I have never screamed before.

At this point I have long since stopped struggling with my emotions. I know that later my regret and remorse are going to eat me from the inside out, but right now, I don't care. I'm gasping for breath as my fingers feather lightly over my pulsing clit while Trent's movements set off every nerve ending in my body.

"The walls of your sweet pussy feel so damn good when my balls hit your ass, babe."

He pulls almost all the way out and then slams in again, stilling himself. It causes me to lose my balance and fall forward on the bed. Without missing a beat he hauls me back up by the waist and continues drilling into me, harder and faster now, hitting every sensitive spot I have.

I almost feel a 'pop' as the pressure that has been building up inside me explodes. An overwhelming feeling passes through my body like a warm and powerful wave and I cry out. Trent continues his heartless assault on my aching pussy, fucking me for reasons known to only him. He's relentless as he keeps going and going.

"FUCKING HELL!" he roars as I feel him detonate as well.

He kisses me feverishly all along my shoulders and upper back, languidly circling his semi-hard dick inside me.

I collapse onto the bed and he goes down with me, losing our connection. All of a sudden, I feel his fingers spreading me wide as he inserts two. The unexpected intrusion makes me flinch. His fingers glide lazily in and out while neither of us speaks a word.

My eyes go wide as I realize what it is he is doing. He's marking me! His fingers aren't in me for my pleasure; they're in me because he doesn't want his seed to come out.

I'm brought back to Earth by the sickening recollection that the fingers coaxing and soothing me are not my husband's fingers; they are the fingers of another man. I've just allowed myself to be fucked like a damn dog in heat.

A warm, putrid feeling erupts in my mouth, and a burning sensation forms in my throat. Oh, Jesus, get him off me and make him stop. I am so thankful that he cannot see the torment and disgust written all over my face.

Lying here with his arms now securely around me in the middle of a warm Atlanta afternoon, a lonely tear slips past my defenses as I try to picture my Turner being the one holding me. It's impossible. I can't, because the one who is pressed up against me and holding me so possessively looks exactly like him.

"You doing okay?" he finally asks.

"Wonderful," I lie through clenched teeth.

"I seem to lose all control of myself with you, Clove. It's like you've hijacked my fucking brain and it's screaming at my cock to bury itself inside you. I need my daily fix of you. You have no idea how lo . . ."

He almost slipped and gave something away! What the hell was he going to say? A plan enters my jumbled mess of a brain. I am not the type of woman to just sit here and let my brother do all of the work, so tonight, I am going to push this crazy, distorted excuse for a human being into hell with me and see how he fucking likes it.

Chapter Eight

He's fallen asleep beside me and I can hear the faint sounds of his snoring. I lift his arm off of me and place it back down as carefully as I can, then roll to the side of the bed and withdraw myself from it.

I spin on my heel and look down at him. I'm no better than this manipulating, screwed up asshole is, I think to myself as my gaze travels up and down my bed. Turner's bed. Our bed. I want to burn it, burn it with this piece of shit lying here naked with a smug look on his face as he sleeps. I hate him. Not as much as I hate myself right now for what I let him do to me, but I still fucking hate him.

I turn and rush into the bathroom, smacking my elbow into the doorframe, not even caring about the pain that is now flaring up my arm. I welcome it. I deserve it. I deserve every ounce of the pain that is hitting me everywhere.

Stepping into the shower, I turn on the hot tap but a blast of cold water hits me across my face and the front of my body. I still don't care. I shiver and shake, sinking to the bottom. The overwhelming pressure lets loose as I curl myself up in a ball on my side.

Oh God, I so wish I could run to my father and tell him everything. I just want him to hold me in his arms and tell me that everything is going to be all right. And yet I know I can't. He wouldn't be able to control himself like Zack; no, my dad would grab his shotgun and kill that beast for the simple fact that I am hurting.

I am suddenly aware that extremely hot water is pelting my skin, stinging my backside. I gradually stand up and adjust the water to a comfortable temperature.

With shaky hands, I reach for the soap and begin to scrub my body everywhere, placing particular attention on my most private area. I need him off of me a-fucking-gain, and no matter how much I scrub and try to cleanse myself, he's still there.

He's never going to come off of me, ever, so I stop just before I tear off my skin from rubbing so hard and stand under the spray to rinse away what I can of him.

I look down to see the last bit of suds escaping down the drain, so I shut the water off. I stand there for a few more minutes trying to gather my thoughts before stepping out and grabbing a towel from the towel holder that is built into the wall. It's yet another reminder of Turner's thoughtful design when we hired the contractors to redo the bathroom.

He is literally everywhere in this house, and suddenly, I can't take it anymore. I can't do this. I just can't. I need to get out of here and help my brother find the only man that I will ever love and just hope like hell that he is able to forgive me for everything I have done.

I quickly brush my hair and pull the wet strands back into a ponytail. I apply lotion all over my body and add just a little bit of a shiny gloss to my lips. Without even taking a glance at Trent laying on the bed, I grab some clean panties and bra out of my dresser, then step into my closet and grab the first thing I lay my hands on. It turns out to be a very old, pale pink sundress. I pull it over my head, adjusting the straps as I walk out of the room, closing the door behind me.

I practically fly down the stairs in a frenzy, snatching my phone from the counter and stepping outside into the blistering Atlanta summer heat. I adjust one of the patio chairs to face the door so I can watch for signs that Trent is about to appear. Plopping myself into it, I swipe my phone and take a deep breath before hitting Zack's number. I hold the phone up to my ear.

"Please answer," I whisper.

After three rings it goes to voicemail. I know my voice sounds shaky and scared as I leave my message.

"Zack. I- I don't think I can do this for much longer. Please call me back, and please tell me you have found some answers."

I disconnect the call and toss my phone on the patio table. Leaning forward, I place my face in my hands and my shoulders sag in defeat. I don't know how long I stay that way as I try and calm my racing brain and my aching heart. The sound of my phone ringing is what brings me back. It's Krista calling. When I answer, I am greeted by Krista's frantic voice.

"Oh dear God, Clove! I have been trying to call you for over an hour, please tell me you're doing okay," she begs.

"I don't know, Krista. I feel like I don't know anything, anymore. This is a nightmare and I can't seem to wake up no matter how hard I try."

She must hear the frantic shakiness in my voice because she starts crying.

"Krista, don't cry. Please."

"I don't know what else to do, Clove. Don't keep all of this to yourself. You know I am always here for you. Always. Right?"

"I know you are, and I love you even more for it." And I do love her. All this has been dumped on her just like the rest of us. "You just had a baby and the best thing you can do for me right now is to take care of yourself and my handsome little nephew."

After a few moments, her sobs start to subside and a small laugh escapes from her mouth.

"He is quite handsome, isn't he?" she says with pride.

"He's the best."

I close my eyes and images of my nephew with all of his hair and big eyes come to my mind, making me feel somewhat more peaceful.

I wish I had the ability right now to be able to talk to Krista face to face about my feelings. Not really knowing how long I have been out here or when Trent is going to wake up, Krista and I make plans. She is going to call me first thing in the morning and ask if I want to go shopping with her and the baby

I really need someone to talk to about all of this, someone besides my brother, who I cannot tell the most intimate details of what is happening between Trent and me. I need someone who I know will not look at me with pity because that is the last thing I need right now. I need someone who can help me get through this, and Krista is that someone.

An inexplicable unease creeps all the way up my spine when I enter back into the house. Gripping my phone tightly, I walk across the kitchen floor and stand at the bottom of the stairs. I hear Trent's voice and yet I cannot make out his words, as they are muted and distant. I stand there for several minutes debating whether or not to climb the stairs and try to listen in. Before I know it, my feet are moving ever so slowly up until I hear his muffled words.

"I don't give a shit." He pauses. "Dad. I have to go before she comes back in here."

Dad? Are you fucking kidding me? Their dad? What the hell is going on? How any of them could be so fucked up as to do what they are doing is beyond me. My eyes go wide and I don't have time to think as I hear him walking out of my room and making his way down the hall. I leap two stairs at a time and skid into the kitchen across the hardwood floor, almost falling on my ass in the process.

"Clove, babe." His voice echoes from behind me just as I am reaching up to pull a glass out of the cupboard. I compose my unsteady voice as best I can.

"In here."

"You wore me out."

His gaze searches my face while his hand rubs across his chin. I don't give a thing away as I stand there calm and collected and drain the contents of my glass of water.

"You're a little red. Were you outside?" he asks casually, his eyes never leaving my face.

"Yeah. I was out back sitting in the sun and kind of lost track of time."

I turn and set my glass in the sink and walk his way until I am standing directly in front of him. I cannot seem to read his thoughts. Roaming my hands up his chest and around his neck until my hands clasp together, I kiss him tenderly on the lips.

"So I wore you out, huh?" I smile as I pull myself back an inch or so.

"You're a smart ass, you know that?"

He places his hands on my hips and closes the small space between us.

"Who? Me?" I shrug. His smile widens. "I just find it funny, is all."

"Is that right?"

"It is. I could have sworn you said you were going to fuck me raw. Which you did, by the way. However, I do find it funny that you're the one who got worn out."

"We'll see who wears whom out later then."

He releases his grip and with a slight swagger to his walk, he moves past me to open the fridge. He grabs a beer, twisting the cap off and flicking it into the sink before taking a healthy swig. Satisfied, he sets it down on the counter then leans back and crosses his arms over his naked chest.

"So, lazy day today then, huh? You're sure you don't want to go out?"

Hell, no, I don't want to go out with him!

"We can go out if you really want to."

"Nah. I think I would much rather stay home and have my wife all to myself."

His eyes rake over my body savagely, raging with fire.

There is no way he is touching me again, so I walk to the small wine cabinet and pull out my first bottle of wine of the day. I don't care if it is the middle of the afternoon, I plan on being drunk by dinnertime and passing my ass out. The thing is, while the thought of him touching me again has my skin itching all over, the worst part is the fact that I want him to.

****

"You're drunk."

Trent leans into me as we sit side by side on the couch, his lips close to mine.

"So?" I ask. And then hiccup.

"You're cute when you're drunk."

I frown.

"And I'm not when I'm sober?" I inch my face farther away from his.

We have been sitting here watching some shoot-em-up action movie for the past few hours and now the credits are rolling on the giant flat screen television sitting above the fireplace. It hasn't been used since last winter when Turner and I . . . no, I can't let my mind wander like that, not when I am drunk like this or I may give myself away.

"You're more than cute when you're sober, Clove, and you know it."

He says the last part as if I'm some stuck up snob. I wrinkle my nose.

"I don't think I'm cute, you ass."

"Well, you are." He grazes his hands down my bare legs. "Your legs are so smooth and long. You're gorgeous, Clove."

His voice sounds so sincere. Even in my drunken state, I can tell that lies and deceit come easily for him. He smoothes his hand back up my leg in languid circles, stopping at the edge of my dress which comes to a few inches above my knees. Keeping his gaze fixated on his every move, he scales up over my dress and leisurely over my stomach and breasts until he reaches my face.

He caresses my cheek as if he is memorizing every single one of my features then runs his hand around to the back of my neck and up into my hair, which is now out of its pony tail and hanging loosely down my back. My body goes weak as he pulls his fingers through the strands from root to tip and then back up again. The feeling is pleasurable and so calming that I close my eyes and drift. It is such a loving gesture that I can't help but melt. I need to gain my strength back and get away from his hypnotizing words and hands.

"You really are exquisitely beautiful, Clove," he whispers.

I lean my head back against the couch and his hands drop from my hair.

"You really know how to sober a girl up," I say breathlessly.

"Not my intention at all, babe. Just speaking the truth."

We stare into each other's eyes for several seconds, and fuck if I don't see just a smidge of remorse there. For some reason Trent seems to have a soft spot when it comes to me. I can see it painfully trying to break out while he sits here and stares at me.

He's a riddle that I can't seem to figure out, and then I see pain in his expression and I understand even less. Is he being forced to do this? And by who? His father? I glance away from him to look up at the clock and see that it's dinnertime.

"You hungry?"

I try and read his expression when I look back at him but it's blank as he stares at the television.

"Yeah. I could eat."

"I'll go call us in something, then."

Shifting my body so I can stand, I grab my empty wine glass and his empty beer bottle and make my way into the kitchen. I set both items down on the counter and with shaky hands I pour myself another glass of wine, downing the entire glass before pouring another. I set the second glass on the counter and after calling for the takeout, I send a quick text off to my brother.

WHERE IN THE HELL ARE YOU?

Almost instantly my phone rings, and when I look at the screen and see it's Zack, my heart leaps out of my chest. I lift the phone to my ear, but before I even get the chance to say hello, it's snatched out of my hand and I am pinned to the counter by Trent's large frame as he answers the phone in my place.

"Hey, bro. What's up?"

Chapter Nine

Pale with desolation, I stand there trapped as his hands roam freely, his fingers tweaking my nipples. I am beyond pissed at him. Turner would never disrespect me in that way and snatch my phone from my hands. This is only further proof of how different Trent is from my husband. What a fucking pig. Nudging him away from me, I move past him and head up the stairs knowing there is no hope of being able to talk to my brother now.

Does Trent suspect that I know? No. How could he? Or, maybe he does, and that is why he snatched the phone from me. It's strange because this man has done his homework. He knows full well that Zack is a detective, yet he still took over my husband's identity.

I enter my room and throw myself on my bed. Trent follows soon after in a temper.

"What the hell is wrong with you, Clove?"

"You took the phone right out of my hand, Turner."

I'm jumpy as hell on the inside but I will not kowtow to this animal. He rakes his hand through his jet-black hair as if frustrated.

"Jesus Christ. I just wanted to see if he wanted to play some basketball tomorrow."

"I'm sorry, then. Did he by chance tell you why he was calling?" I trail off vaguely.

"Yes, he did." He plops his big body on the bed with a heavy bounce. "I guess your dad is coming over tomorrow night for dinner, so he was calling to invite us, too."

His lips part in a good-humored smile. Shit. My dad! How in the hell am I supposed to act normally in front of my dad? This is driving me insane and not being able to talk to Zack until tomorrow is making it worse.

I loathe this man lying here on my marital bed . . . the bed where I willingly let him take me. The fact that I loved it makes me just as sick and fucked up as he is.

This is wrong, so damn wrong. I am sitting here playing house with a monster. I have to find a way to be able to talk to my brother or the only way I am going to be able to sleep tonight is to drink a hell of a lot more wine than I have in this house.

Fucking prick, I think to myself as I smile back.

"Didn't mean to upset you, babe. Now, come on. I'll give in and sit through one of your stupid chick flicks if you forgive me."

He looks at me with childlike eyes and on the inside I am laughing my damn ass off. If he really was Turner then he would know that I am not a chick flick kind of girl. I am a horror movie girl. I'll humor him, though.

"I'm not in the mood for a chick flick tonight. How about we find the scariest movie we can find and watch that instead?" I lift my brows in challenge.

"Let's go, then." He climbs off the bed. "I'll even be a nice husband and let you pick it out." His voice trails behind him as he goes down the stairs.

You do that, asshole, because while I am sitting there watching it, I am going to pretend it's me who shoots you through your black fucking soul in the end.

****

I feel nauseated and my head is pounding. I am damn near parched to death as I lay here at eleven o'clock in the damn morning. Rolling over to my side and noticing the empty spot next to me, tears prick my eyes when I think about the fact that I have slept another night without Turner.

I miss him so much. Wanting him back here with me, I let the tears fall silently. I deserve this pain I am feeling and so much more. Curling myself up in a tight ball, I cry helplessly for the man I love. My head is hurting so bad from the wine I consumed last night, but my heart hurts even more.

"Please come back to me safely," I plead as I rub the side of the bed where he usually sleeps. "I don't want to live my life without you, but I will as long as I know you're alive and well."

I'm so afraid that something has happened to him and he is never going to come back.

Making up my mind to crawl out of bed, I fling the covers off and notice that I am completely naked. I never sleep naked. My stomach rolls at the fact that Trent must have brought me to bed because the last thing I remember was passing out at the very end of the movie.

"Shit," I mumble.

Why do you even care if he saw you naked, you filthy slut? You slept with him knowing he isn't your husband and you loved it!

Despite the fact that my head is pounding, I jump out of bed and make a mad dash for the bathroom. Landing on my knees in front of the toilet, I vomit everything in my stomach and gag with the dry heaves even after nothing else comes up.

I shake, beads of sweat forming on my forehead. I lay my head on the tile floor and thank God Trent is gone playing basketball so he doesn't see me falling apart like this. My brother has got to be climbing out of his damn skin knowing he is playing ball with a colossal fake.

Right then it hits me.

He's gone.

I jump up quickly and have to steady myself as a wave of dizziness hits me full force. Once I feel somewhat normal, I lift my head and look at myself in the mirror.

What a fucking mess. I can't even stand to look at myself. So, I don't. I turn the water on and once it is hot enough for me to stand under, I get my hair washed and my body scrubbed clean in less than ten minutes.

I need to hurry. I have no clue what time he is going to be back, so I grab all my clothes and dress in a rush. I head into Turner's closet in hopes of finding some sort of clue without Trent noticing I was in here. After several minutes of looking through every possible thing I can find, I come up empty handed. I make sure everything is back the way I found it and head toward the dresser and rummage through everything there, too.

I keep searching the entire bedroom. Nothing. Sitting down on the edge of the bed, I try to think. If I wanted to hide something from someone in here, where would I put it? My eyes desperately scan the room and then suddenly stop at the picture of Turner and me on top of my dresser. Something draws me to it, my feet moving of their own accord. I brush my hand over Turner's face before I pick it up and turn it over. When I lift the hinges on the back, I smirk when I see a small folded up piece of paper lying against the picture.

My hands tremble as I pick it up and set the frame back down on the dresser. Opening it as fast as I can, I am shocked when I see a picture placed neatly inside. It's old and faded, and yet I can still make out that it's a family photo. Melody is sitting on a bench holding one of the twins while a man who I have never seen before is holding the other.

Studying the man's features, I know he must be Turner's father as his features are so similar to both of the twins'; black hair, chiseled nose, and that very prominent square chin. Turner and Trent look so much alike I cannot tell them apart. I stare at the man who helped bring my husband into this world and wonder what he and Trent are doing and what they seem to think they will gain by destroying Turner's life.

I set the photo down on the dresser and open the piece of paper and right there in black ink is an address and phone number that I would recognize anywhere- they're Melody's. The ten million dollar question is; what is Trent doing with it, and why?

After running down to the kitchen and grabbing my phone off the charger, I sprint back up the stairs and take a screenshot of the family photo and then make sure to put everything back in its proper place. I go about making the bed and brushing my teeth and applying as much makeup as I can to my face to hide the dark circles under my eyes without going overboard

Just as I am finishing up with blow-drying my hair, I hear the front door slam shut and Trent jogging up the stairs. Taking a deep, calming breath, I stroll out of the bathroom and into the bedroom just as he enters.

"How was basketball?"

I pour on the kindness.

"It was all right. Forgot how good your brother actually is, though. He kicked my ass."

Shrugging off his drenched t-shirt and tossing it onto the floor, he comes further into the bathroom.

"He always kicks your ass. Did you forget he played ball in college?"

"No. I didn't forget." He slips off his shorts and tosses them onto the floor, too.

I force my gaze away from him because the sight of him makes me sick. He steps into the shower to turn it on and I wait a few minutes to make sure he's under the spray before I speak again.

"Are you hungry?" I ask.

"Starving but your brother said to stop over any time we want to so I don't want to eat too much."

"Okay."

I close the door behind me and with my phone in my hand I have Zack's number dialed and the phone pressed to my ear before I even hit the bottom of the stairs.

"Thank Christ," he answers.

"Zack. I don't have much time and I need to know what you found out yesterday?"

"Clove. First off, you have no idea how much I wanted to wrap my hands around that piece of scum's neck and squeeze every last ounce of his breath out of him this morning. Fucker talks to me last night and this morning like he's my best fucking friend."

"I know exactly how you feel. I am living with him, remember? Now please give me something. Anything to help me ease my mind."

His sudden silence is intolerably irksome.

"Zack?"

"I'm here, Clove. I need to tell you everything and I won't do it over the phone."

"Zack. I am hanging by a thread, here. God, do you know what I let him do to me yesterday? Do you have any idea what this is doing to me at all?" I have never had to beg my brother for anything in my entire life, but I do now. "Please, Zack?"

"I'm sorry. I just, I am trying to do this with my head and not my heart, trying to treat this just like every other missing person's case and not my brother-in-law. I am doing this the way I was taught. It's the only way I can do it, Clove. Shove my personal feelings aside and do my job. By the way, Melody was just as shocked as you were when I told her everything, but one thing I can tell you is that she believes it's their father who is orchestrating this entire thing."

"I know that already. I overheard Trent talking to their dad yesterday. Is Melody all right?"

My heart flutters with terror for what my mother-in-law must be going through.

"Hell, no. She's not all right. And what the hell did you hear him to say his dad? Fuck, this is an investigation, Clove. When you find something out, you need to call and tell me this shit."

How dare my brother talk all pissy like this to me?

"I was going to tell you about it, I just never got the chance and you know it."

"Shit, sis. I'm sorry. Just, from now on if you suspect anything at all, please find a way to let me know. Okay?"

"Okay," I cry.

"Now look, there is so much that I have to tell you. Somehow we have to sneak off tonight. That was why when Trent answered the phone last night I said I was calling to have you two over for dinner. Dad really was planning on coming over, anyway."

"That's another thing. It's going to be very hard to convince dad that I am doing fine. You know he can smell a lie a mile away."

My heart breaks even more thinking about how my dad is going to feel when he finds out the truth.

"We'll figure something out together."

I hear the shower turn off and move to the fridge to get everything out to make a sandwich.

"Zack, I have to go. He's coming."

"Be safe, and get over here as soon as you can. I love you."

"Love you, too. Bye."

Hanging up the phone and deleting the last call, I set it back on the counter and make a turkey and cheese on rye sandwich. Turner hates rye bread so let's see if dear ole Trent hates it too.

I grab a handful of chips that I pull out of the pantry and set it on the table along with the half of a sandwich I made for myself.

"Thanks." Trent sits down at the table next to me a few minutes later and takes a giant bite of his sandwich.

"This is so good. I had no idea how hungry I actually was until I stood underneath the shower."

He takes another bite and finishes it off before I even have two bites gone from mine.

"Glad you liked it," I say with a hint of sarcasm in my voice.

He may have done his homework, but he sure as hell didn't do it right. *You fucking failed, asshole.* He doesn't even seem to notice as he gets up from the table and places his dishes in the sink.

"You were out cold last night," he says, wrapping his arms around my neck from behind and kissing the side of my temple.

"I know. It must have been all that wine."

He releases his hold and I continue to stare forward, feeling as if I am barely breathing at this point as he stands behind me. Tilting my neck back so I can see him, he looks down at me with eyes so potent and full of lust and want.

"Turn around, babe," he commands, his voice low and gravelly.

What is he going to do? He couldn't have heard me on the phone. No. He wants something, I can tell by the look in his eyes. Oh my God. He's on a sexual mission to destroy me and here I am incapable of doing anything to stop him.

I keep repeating over and over in my head that I am doing this out of love for my husband, and I am. But when Trent looks at me like that . . . how can I truly be doing this out of love for one man when I allow another to bring me pleasure?

He must think I am taking too long, because he bends down and lifts the chair on his own. Before I know it, I am facing him and staring directly at the thick, hard bulge right in front of my face. Kneeling before me so his face is even with mine, he guides himself between my legs. I have no choice but to spread them, making room for his large frame.

"You are so flawless. I could look at you all day, Clove."

When I look into his eyes, something tells me that he truly believes what he is saying as he takes in my face and moves his gaze down my neck.

"I need to taste you so bad right now, Clove. I'm fucking craving that sweet pussy right now."

He's on his knees now as he positions himself exactly the way he wants and runs his hands up and down my legs, pushing my dress higher and higher as he goes until it's bunched up and my white lace thong is showing. Until now, he hasn't taken his eyes off my face this entire time, but when he sees what he says he is craving, his tongue darts out and he licks his lips as he puts his hands under my ass and pulls me forward in the chair.

My hands instantly go to the wooden arms of the chair to support myself.

"Hang on tight, babe. I am not messing around right now. I am going to fuck this pussy with my fingers and my mouth and just when you think you have had enough, I am going to dive right back in for more." He rips my thong off and drops it to the floor. "As far as I am concerned, *this* is the most important meal of my fucking day."

Lowering his head to within an inch of my core, he takes a deep breath and blows softly, sending a thrill of excitement through my nerves that starts there and shoots all the way to my brain. Everything goes blurry and numb. When he takes his first long, slow lick, I squirm in the chair. With his hands tightening even more on my ass, he grins satisfactorily and nips at my clit with his teeth. He keeps it up until I lay my head back and clench the sides of the chair tightly.

I can't get the image of what this man is doing to me out of my head and escape my shame. And no matter how hard I try to not give him the satisfaction of knowing his talented mouth is bringing me pleasure, I can't.

It's building and building and then I scream and curse and twitch and I hardly even recognize my own name when he calls it out as I climax all over his face. But I don't allow myself to look at him when his mouth leaves my pussy. I keep my head titled back and my eyes closed, trying to catch my breath.

"You're so fucking hot sitting there completely vulnerable and so damn sexy. I love you, Clove." He chuckles and leans over me so I have to open my eyes.

"I love you too, Turner," I say in a stupefied voice.

He stares at me for a very long time before he stands up straight. I follow him with my gaze.

"I have a little business to take care of in the office before we go," he says as he turns and walks away from me.

"Anything I can help with?"

"No, I got it. It should only take a few hours and then we can head over to your brother's house. Holler at me if you need me," he calls out as he heads down the hall and shuts the door to my husband's office.

He thinks I have no damn clue what the hell is going on. I hope he's so fucking hard his balls fall off. He's infuriating as hell. He eats me out like he has to have it and then turns around and goes into Turner's office to do God knows what. As for me, I am no better than he is as I sit here and look at myself. I hate myself and I hate whatever the fuck is going on here.

I finally walk into the half bathroom off of the kitchen and clean myself up. Then I head down to the laundry room and get a clean pair of panties out of the dryer to put on.

Without even giving it a second thought, I snatch my phone and keys off of the counter and get in my car. I'm all set to leave, that is, until I look behind me and see my mother-in-law pulling in the driveway.

Chapter Ten

"Melody. What in the hell are you doing here?"

Bitterness and betrayal drip from my voice and I can tell she senses it by the way she takes a step back.

"I- I don't know, Clove."

Her eyes dart around, looking everywhere except at me.

"You don't know? For Christ's sake, Melody. Do you have any idea whatsoever what is happening here? Did Zack not explain everything to you? If Trent sees you out here we may never find Turner. You need to leave now," I hiss, pointing to her car and indicating for her to get back in and go.

"I'm his mother, too. Maybe, just maybe, I can talk some sense into him; find out where Turner is. Please, I just need to see him. I have lived with this nightmare for twenty-six years not knowing where my son is. I'm his *mother*."

Is she shitting me right now? I stick my face inches from hers.

"Listen here, Melody. I know you're his mother and you're also my husband's mother, but that man in there is a damn stranger to all of us. If you care about Turner at all, you will get back in your damn car and leave until you either hear back from Zack or me. I can't imagine what you're going through right now, but you know what? I really don't give two flying fucks, because as far as I am concerned everything that is happening here is your fault!"

"Look, sweetheart. I know you're upset-"

"*Upset?* I am way more than 'upset.' I have no idea if my husband is dead or alive and I am sleeping with a fucking stranger who could be a murderer as far as I know, so yeah, Melody. I am *fucking upset!*"

I am trying to stay as calm as I can and not raise my voice too loud to cause a scene. Part of me feels for what Melody is going through right now. I can tell by her stature and the puffiness in her eyes that she has been crying, and most likely hasn't slept since hearing the news. But the truth is that I have no sympathy whatsoever for the woman standing in front of me.

"You haven't talked to your brother, have you?"

I hear the rawness in her voice and I know this has to be a shock to her, but until I know exactly what is going on here and why, I need her to leave.

"Not in depth," I say briskly, "So I have no clue what is happening. Now excuse me for being so blunt, but I don't give a shit how you feel. The sight of you right now makes me sick, Melody. I have no clue where my husband is . . . the man you raised. *He's* the one we need to be concerned about right now, not that man inside my house. Now leave, and you'd better hope like fucking hell that my Turner . . ."

My voice cracks and I start to shed unwanted tears.

"My Turner is okay, because so help me God, if he's not there will never be an excuse good enough from you."

She just stands there in shock while pear-shaped tears rapidly slide down her face. As I watch her climb into her car and back out of my driveway, I realize that what sucks most of all is that I couldn't bring myself to console her in any way. I just can't comprehend what reason a mother would have for keeping this kind of secret, but no matter why she has done it, I don't know if I will ever be able to forgive her.

Most women would envy my relationship with my mother-in-law. She has always been the mother that I never had and I love her more than anything. Acting like a cold-hearted bitch when I was talking to her doesn't make me feel any better at all.

When I first found out about all this, I wanted to lash out at her in more ways than one. Now, after seeing the look on her face and knowing she is hurting just as badly as I am, I feel terrible for the words I said to her. I simply can't risk Trent finding out everything yet, not until I know Turner is safe. With her being so unstable and not having seen her other son since he was a toddler, she would most likely ruin everything, no matter what she says.

I make my way back into the house with my head down and walking at a snail's pace, the tension and fearfulness taking over as I try and reassure myself Trent didn't see or hear her in the driveway. When I approach the garage my eyes roam everywhere to try and find some sort of weapon to use just in case he is inside and attacks me when I enter.

Finding a wrench in a small red toolbox that Turner keeps in the far back corner of the garage, I creep slowly towards the door leading into the house and turn the handle uneasily. Once inside, I gently close it behind me and peer down the hallway toward the office, noticing the door is still closed.

Needing to make sure he is still in there, I stealthily progress down the hall until I am nearly in front of the door and stop. The sound of what appears to be an e-mail or some other sort of notification on the computer is all I hear, and then fingers fluently tapping away as if they were e-mailing back.

A sigh of relief escapes as I turn and tiptoe like a burglar back into the kitchen while wondering who the hell he is e-mailing. More than likely it's his dickhead of a father. I could spit nails at that man. Better yet, I could blow both his and his heartless son's fucking brains out and not give a second thought about it if it would bring Turner back to me safe and unharmed.

Becoming aware that I still have the wrench clasped tightly in my hand, I exit the kitchen and climb the stairs to the bedroom where I place the wrench underneath the mattress on my side of the bed.

Living through what I am right now has my mind drifting back to an earlier conversation with Zack. He told me Turner would not want me to feel the way I am feeling now, and that he would want me safe. I am keeping the wrench right there, and the next time Trent tries to touch me . . . I will use it.

I smooth out the comforter and sit down on the end of the bed facing the window, where the sun is shining through so brightly that the beams glisten from hitting the full-length mirror in the corner. I lift my head and stare at my wedding picture. My thoughts drift to so many memories that the two of us shared. Vacations. Walks where we would hold hands and talk about our future plans, or sometimes even just walk in silence enjoying each other's company.

Turner and I were just in the beginning stages of talking about having children. We both wanted to wait until we had our feet solidly planted on the ground financially before we brought a child into this world. He was so adamant about me being a stay at home mom that at first we argued about it. But, the more I thought about it, the more I wanted to stay home and be the best mom I could be.

Taking our children to soccer practice, swim lessons . . . it didn't matter what they did. We wanted to be those parents whose child knew how much their mom and dad loved them, and would never feel the emptiness in their hearts of being abandoned as both Turner and I felt when we were growing up. We have both been betrayed by a parent, and now it seems that Turner is being betrayed by both.

"Clove, are you up there?" Trent hollers from the bottom of the stairs.

"Yeah. I'm changing my clothes."

Pushing myself up from the bed, I go pull out yet another summer sundress from my closet to put on.

"I'm all done and set to go."

His voice doesn't sound like he suspects anything, yet I still tremble as I take my dress off and step into the other one and zip it up at the side.

"I'll be down in a minute," I call. "Just freshening up a little."

I assess my appearance in the bathroom mirror. Looking at the reflection staring back at me, I barely recognize myself as I truly take myself in for the first time in a long while. I see confusion, not simplicity. I see dullness and not vibrancy in my eyes. I see a woman who doesn't even know who she is anymore. I see a scared, bitter, and angry woman all mixed into one.

No, the woman staring back at me is not Clove Calloway, wife of Turner Calloway. The woman staring back at me is someone I don't recognize at all. A woman who I hate just as much as I hate the man downstairs. I am a sham of a woman, an imposter just like he is, and fuck if I know if I will ever be able to get that vibrant, simplistic woman back ever again.

"Wow. You look breathtaking, babe."

Trent's observation of my appearance stops me dead in my tracks when I enter the kitchen. He sounds so sincere and his phrase is exactly like one Turner would use.

"Thank you, big boy," I reply, doing my best to mask my anger.

His intangible charm does nothing for my sour mood at all. However, I feel all of the strain and pressure leave my body as he seems like he knows nothing about his mother's short visit. I don't know if he is playing me for a bigger fool than I already am. He could know, or at least suspect that I know, who he really is and is waiting for the right time to plan his attack and strike.

In a short while I will have to face another parent who knows absolutely nothing about what is going on. I need to think long and hard before we get to my brother's house about how I am going to make sure it stays that way.

Unlike Melody, my dad won't listen to a word anyone has to say if he finds out. He would come unglued and kill this bastard for what he is doing to this family.

I'm completely stressed out and about ready to hit my breaking point the closer we get to my brother's house. I try to stay as normal as I possibly can while sitting here listening to Trent carry on a conversation, at this point with himself, as all I am doing is answering with yes, no, and maybe. He pummels me with all sorts of questions which mostly shoot right over the top of my head. All I can think about is being able to somehow get alone with my brother without Trent becoming suspicions or my father wanting to be a part of our conversation.

Pulling onto Zack and Krista's street and seeing my dad's car already in the driveway only makes my anxiety flare up even more. We park along the curb in front of their house at which point I plaster on a fake smile and open the car door to get out. Trent does the same on his side and when he rounds the car; I grab his hand just like I would normally do if he were Turner as we make our way up the driveway.

I can do this. I have to do this for the safety of my father. The less people who know about this, the better. Who knows what Trent or his father would do to anyone who gets in the way of whatever they want with us? If anything happened to my dad because of this, I could never forgive myself. I put everything in the back of my mind as we knock briefly then just walk inside.

"There she is!"

My dad is up and off of the couch before we even have the door closed, heading in my direction.

"Hi, Dad."

He reaches his arms out and embraces me in his warm and safe hug. For a brief moment I feel safe and sound. It doesn't last long as he tears himself away from me and places his arm around my shoulder while he greets his supposed son-in-law with a handshake.

Returning his attention back to me, he scowls. I scowl back.

"What?" I ask, my smile never faltering.

"You look different, somehow."

"Different? I'm fine, Dad," I wave him off with my hand.

"You look tired. You're not getting enough rest, are you?" he asks, worry etched across his face.

"She had a little too much to drink last night, James," Trent interrupts.

Dad tries to act tough and scold me.

"Girl, I told you that shit isn't good for you."

"Oh, is that right? Let me see; is that your glass of bourbon sitting on the table over there?" I tease as I turn and head further into the house where Zack is holding the baby.

"You sassing me, girl?" Dad jokes from behind me.

All of us laugh at that one, knowing very well that one thing you do not do is sass James Wright. Dad was never cruel to us at all when we were growing up, but he did teach us to respect others and to never ever take anything for granted. And I thought I hadn't, until a few days ago when my life fell apart. Now, standing here looking into the innocent eyes of my nephew, I wonder if I will ever be able to tell Turner that my feelings went from 'like' to 'love' the first time he kissed me, and that he is the greatest joy in my life.

"Clove." Zack nudges me with his shoulder. "Snap out of it before Dad really starts to suspect something."

"Can I hold him, please?"

I'm finding it hard to speak. Even trying to hold a conversation with an adult right now is the last thing I want to do until I get my shit together. Holding and cuddling baby Nolan is exactly what I need to fill my aching heart with love.

I take him from my brother's arms and he stretches and looks up at me. For the first time in days, my smile is as honest as it's ever going to get.

He's so innocent and has no idea what is happening all around him. Not a care in the world. I totally block out all the sounds around me as I stare at him intently, wondering if I will ever have the chance to be a mother.

Chapter Eleven

"So when are you two going to make me a grandpa?" My dad blurts out in the middle of dinner.

My eyes dart around the table. Krista's face has turned white and my brother's jaw starts twitching and clenching.

"Um. I don't really know, Dad. We really haven't talked much about it lately,"

I say meekly as I look down at my dinner. Suddenly, I've lost my appetite.

"I'm thinking we need to start talking about it, and soon," Trent says.

My eyes about bulge out of my head. He reaches down for his beer and takes a long swig, then points the bottle at where Krista is sitting, holding baby Nolan while she tries to eat. He puts his arm around me and hugs me to him.

"Seeing the way my girl here was off in baby la-la land earlier when she was holding him got me thinking the same thing, James."

"And what's that?" My lips pull into a tight line.

"Just that I was watching you and picturing in my mind how you would look pregnant with our child. And knowing that you're carrying the next generation of Calloways."

A lump forms in my throat and I bite my tongue to suppress what I really want to say. *Hell to the motherfucking no, I will NEVER carry your baby!* The child would most likely be just like him. To my credit, I'm still sitting here with my plastic smile on my face. I lean in and softly place my hand on his cheek, showing my endearment at his words.

Fake. This is all so damn fake, and if I was ever going to have a Calloway baby, it would be with my husband.

A part of me knows now it's never going to happen and my heart breaks all over again with the knowledge. This is all too overwhelming and my head starts whirling. I look at my brother for help, thankful that my dad has gone to place his dishes in the sink.

"Well, I think that's a perfect idea," my dad says as he wipes his hands on the dishtowel and starts loading the dishwasher.

I use that as an excuse to make my escape.

"Here, Dad. Let me get that. You go sit down and enjoy an after dinner drink. Better yet, grab that grandson of yours so Krista can help me. All four of you men scoot out of here and let us clean up."

"Sounds good to me."

My brother hops up from the table and takes the baby from Krista, giving me a knowing look as he passes me by.

"Dad, grab a few beers. Let's turn on the game and give these girls some space out here."

I can tell that my brother's mood has chilled and I sense that Krista feels it too as she gives him a brooding look as he walks away with Nolan in his arms. Trent talks baseball to my dad as they saunter into the living room. Thank God Dad hasn't picked up on any of the tension filling this house today.

It's fucking everywhere. I have seen my brother try through gritted teeth to act like nothing is wrong when he engages in a conversation with Trent. Trent seemingly has been oblivious to it.

As soon as I pick the last plate up off of the table and wander over to the sink, Krista motions for me to come over to where she is standing out of eye and ear shot from the guys.

"Listen, Zack told me to fill you in as much as I could about what's going on, but not here. Let's finish cleaning and then I am going to ask you to go for a walk with me and the baby. I'm sorry the shopping idea didn't go through. After your dad called, we thought this would be a better idea."

"It's fine, really." I wave my hand to signal no big deal.

I clear my throat, all of a sudden finding it very hard to breathe knowing soon I am going to find out what in the hell is really going on. The only thing concerning me right now is that Zack must not be any closer to finding Turner then he was yesterday.

****

It is a mild mid-summer day, perfect for a walk. Zack sets the stroller onto the sidewalk and Krista places Nolan in it, adjusting the top so the sun won't touch him in any way. I become suddenly fascinated with the stroller.

"Geez, these things are like cars."

"They sure are." Krista laughs lightly and places a few diapers along with a blanket, wipes, and whatever else she needs in the small diaper bag she sets underneath the stroller. "They're fully equipped with everything."

I investigate this sucker which has little hidden compartments everywhere. A tinge of jealousy courses through my body when I think of the fact that I may never have the chance to use one of these. It hurts. It hurts so damn bad when I think about this whole fucked up situation and how badly I would give anything to see the look on Turner's face if I were to tell him we were pregnant.

This isn't how life is supposed to be. It sure as hell isn't how I dreamed it would be. What could possibly be the point of Trent and his father doing this? Turner is just your average every day run-of-the-mill guy. He doesn't come from money, so that can't be the reason. What the hell could it be?

"Clove."

I lift my head at hearing my name.

"Shit, Clove, you're crying. Come on."

Krista gently tugs my arm and starts to push the stroller down the sidewalk. I follow and reach up with my hand to swipe away the tears that I didn't even know were falling.

We walk for a couple blocks without either one of us saying anything. I don't know if Krista is giving me the time and space to get my shit together or if it's me who has suddenly become closed off and despondent.

We walk for a few more blocks in silence and turn into the small open patch of grass that has a few wooden benches sitting by the curb.

"Come on, sit." She pats the seat right next to her. I take a seat and lift my head towards the sun as I close my eyes and inhale. "You okay?"

My eyes pop open. Of course I am not okay, but I don't tell her that. I know how worried she is for me and for Turner. So instead I look at her and smile to the best of my ability.

"I just need to know what Melody said," I whisper. Krista stares straight ahead when she speaks next.

"I don't know where to start, really." Her voice cracks with misery.

"Start from the beginning."

At this point, I've given up all hope that they are any closer to finding Turner, because if they were, I know that would have been the first thing out of her mouth the moment we got away from the house.

"Zack said that when he showed up at Melody's without you or Turner, she freaked on him, thinking something had happened to one of you. Once he told her what was happening, it took him almost an hour before she stopped her crying long enough for him to get the entire story out of her." Pausing, she glances my way.

"What the hell happened?"

"James. That's their dad's name." I simply nod and she goes on. "He was an alcoholic and never could keep a job back then. He was very abusive to Melody; they were constantly fighting. Apparently he favored Trent over Turner, she said." We both sharply in take a deep breath at her outburst.

"What?" I exclaim.

"Turner was . . . well, according to Melody anyway, he was always whiny and clumsy, which didn't set well with their father. I guess Trent always did everything first. He got teeth first and learned how to walk first, and Turner was the one who always trailed behind. Whatever she meant by that, I don't know."

She waves her hand in dismissal before continuing.

"Anyway. One day he came home and started in on Turner, and Melody started in on James. She said he snapped and hit her so hard that she fell and hit her head on the edge of their kitchen table. She was knocked out cold, and when she came to he was gone and he had taken Trent with him."

"Oh my God!" I place my hand over my mouth to stifle my scream.

"I know, right? I can't imagine how she must have felt not knowing." Krista lifts her hand and places it gently on Nolan's soft leg as he lays there sleeping.

"Well, what did she do?" I ask.

"She called the cops after a few hours of not hearing anything from him and filed a missing person's report. Zack has a box full of papers and newspaper clippings she gave him. He went through most of them last night and then this morning he took them to the station." Krista places her hand on my knee and squeezes gently.

"They just disappeared, Clove."

My hands fly to my mouth as I think of what Melody has had to go through for the last twenty some-odd years. Christ almighty, I am speechless at this point as my thoughts take over.

I knit my eyebrows together as all of a sudden, confusion abruptly hits. I stand up in a rush and pace a few steps forward before spinning on my heel to face Krista.

"What are you thinking?" She blurts out.

"That gives us a clue as to why he left, but did she say why the hell she kept the kidnapping and the existence of Turner's twin brother from him?" I swing my arms out in question. "She is not telling us everything, Krista. You know, she came by the house earlier today acting all upset and wanting to see Trent. Thank God I was outside and saw her drive up before he did."

"How did she seem?"

"She's hiding something, I just know it. But why? For the life of me I cannot figure out *why*. How in the hell could she live all these years and not say a damn word to anyone? Did the kidnapping investigation just stop? I mean, you don't simply give up trying to find your child!"

Realizing my voice has been getting louder and louder, I take a deep breath and start again in a lower tone.

"No. There is more to this story than she is telling everyone and I am going to find out what the hell it is. She'd better have a damn good reason and tell me the damn truth. My husband is God knows where right now. He could even be de-"

"No! Don't think that, Clove, or even say it." Krista takes hold of both of my hands as she stands. "He's alive. You cannot think that way."

"I don't know anything anymore. If Melody had told him the truth, everything would be fine and my husband would be right here where he belongs. This is too much. What if he's with his piece of shit dad and is being beaten and tortured? Oh God. I need him back."

My entire body starts to shake as I see a vision in my mind of a bloody and beaten Turner being tortured somewhere all alone.

"Stop it right now!" Krista chastises me. "You need to be strong for both you and Turner, and you need to let Zack and everyone else involved do their jobs."

She's right, I know she is, but I just don't know how much stronger I can get. I am dying my own slow, personal death here. My life is never going to be the same, no matter what happens.

"Let Zack do his job, Clove. You know he loves both you and Turner. It's killing him to see you go through this."

"Well, I feel like I am already dead. I'm numb to everything."

"Oh, Clove. Honey, come here."

Krista sits back down and places her arm around me. I lean my head onto her shoulder.

"Did she say anything else?"

"Not really. But Zack feels the same way as you do about her hiding something. He said he asked her several times why she never told anyone and she just kept saying that she was frightened of James. Zack didn't buy that pathetic excuse for a minute."

We share a long glance.

"I need to talk to her myself," I say. "Maybe once she hears the hell I am living in, she will open up and tell me what we need to know. She's Turner's mother for God's sake, but the way she acted this morning was almost as if she was more concerned about Trent than with trying to find the son she actually raised," I say bitterly.

"True," Krista says as she gets up and turns the stroller around. "We should probably head back so Trent doesn't suspect anything."

"I don't think he does."

Thoughts of this morning's sexual escapades in the kitchen flood my mind. Not wanting to share any of the intimate details with Krista, I stand up as well. We make our way back to their house as the sun is slowly descending on the horizon and birds are chirping all around us.

I will definitely be making a phone call to my dear mother-in-law and when we do meet, she will tell me everything. Melody is the only one who can help us now, and she damn well knows it.

Chapter Twelve

I am dying a thousand deaths inside when we come up to Krista and Zack's home. I used to love coming here. Turner loved coming here. The four of us always had such a good time together. I remember how excited my brother was when he bought this house as a wedding present for Krista. He drove her here blindfolded the morning before their wedding. I'll never forget the surprised look on her face when he took off the blindfold and Turner, my dad, and I were standing out front holding a sign saying, "Welcome to your new home."

Now as it looms closer, my heart rate starts to speed up. My worst enemy is sitting inside that house with my family and only one of them knows the truth. Trent puts on a mighty damn fine job of pretending to be his brother, I will give him credit for that.

I detest him, but myself even more for letting him touch me, control me, make me feel things I shouldn't be feeling with anyone else except the man who put these rings on my finger. I stand there staring at them like I am learning their meaning for the first time. I am locked in my own personal jail and I will never be free. Every waking second makes me hate the person that I have become even more.

"Put your happy face on, Clove." Krista snaps me out of my confusion as she takes a crying Nolan out of his stroller.

"I think someone is getting hungry."

I pat his cute little bottom as Krista places him up on her chest and he nuzzles his mouth towards her breast.

"I think you're right," she coos at him as we enter the house.

Dad is the first one up as we walk through the door.

"Holy shit, that boy has some lungs on him!" my dad exclaims as he tries to get Nolan's attention.

"He's hungry, James, so I'm going to take him to his room to feed and change him."

"All right, dear, but bring him back out here so I can see the little man before I leave. He and I need to have a talk."

"Whatever, Dad. What could you possibly have to discuss with a two week old baby?" I question with a smartass look on my face.

Leave it to my father to put a much-needed smile on my face.

"We need to start talking about me teaching him how to hunt."

His face goes all serious and he pulls his pants up and puffs out his chest.

"You did not just say that shit about my son, Dad."

Zack enters the conversation from across the room where he has his feet propped up on the coffee table and a beer in his hand. His eyes are glued to the baseball game and yet he can still hear my dad.

"I sure as shit did, boy. That kid has a firm grip on those little hands, which means he'll be able to grip a shotgun real damn good."

"My kid is not hunting, Dad. And that grip he's got means he is going to play some ball just like his dad did."

Zack is totally egging my dad on now.

"We'll see about that," Dad says as he takes his seat next to Zack and pats him on the leg.

The two of them bantering back and forth has me thinking how good it is to feel right at home. That is, until I feel arms snake around my middle from behind. Despite it being nice and warm outside, I suddenly go cold all over. The bristle on the back of my neck stands up as he leans his head on my shoulder.

"Hey baby. How was the walk?" He nips at the side of my neck.

"It was great. I feel refreshed and thirsty. I'm going to get some water. Excuse me for a minute."

Trent releases his hands and they drop to his side as he strides back and sits in the chair.

"I need another beer," I hear Zack say as I enter the kitchen.

"Grab me one too, would you, bro?" Trent asks and my eyes grow wide as I think about what Zack must be feeling.

"Dad, you need one?"

"Nah, I'm good. I need to be going soon anyway, and you know two is my limit, son."

I hear what sounds like a pat on the back or shoulder as I stand in the middle of the kitchen like a statue waiting for my brother.

"Mother fucking piece of shit scum bag," Zack mutters softly as he enters the kitchen. "God, Clove. This is fucking torture. You have no idea how much I want to arrest that fucker right now."

Zack quickly darts my way and pulls me in for a hug.

"I know, Zack."

"She told you everything, then?" He says as he steps away and goes straight to the fridge.

"Can you grab me a bottle of water out of there?" I ask a little too loudly.

"Yes, and you and I need to talk. Can you call me first thing in the morning at the office?" I question.

He nods his reply, twisting the caps off of both beers and taking a long, deep swig of his.

"Hang in there, sis. I love you."

"I love you, too." I whisper as he walks away.

For the hundredth time in a matter of days, I go pretend to be the happy little wife even though nothing seems to make me happy. I doubt if I will ever know the true meaning of that word again.

After hugs, kisses, and a promise to call my father for lunch, Trent and I are on our way home. His hands seem to be all over me the minute we hit the interstate and it's making me enormously uncomfortable as his hands roam everywhere.

"We're going to crash if you keep that up, you know."

I'm dripping with enthusiasm on the outside and yet on the inside I am fighting him off with everything that I have. Right at this moment I may be able to tolerate having his hands on me, but at least for tonight I am going to make sure that is as far as he gets.

With each new day I pray that this is the day Turner just walks through our front door, or he calls me and says he is okay. How nice it would be to pull into my driveway and walk into my house and there he is, waiting for me like he would do any other night when I would be out. I know it's not going to happen.

My Turner, my love, and my life is somewhere out there suffering even more so than I am, and the thought of anyone hurting him has my heart numb. I am empty inside. If this is the end of my perfect marriage to the man of my dreams, I know I will not have the strength to move on from the loss of him.

There is no need to pinch myself to see if I am dreaming; this nightmare is so fucking real that it will forever haunt me.

Trent's voice breaks through my thoughts.

"What are you thinking about over there, Clove? Did you even hear a word I said?"

"Eh. Nothing important. Just daydreaming."

"About what?"

He keeps his head facing the road while his hand continues to roam up and down my thigh. I need to think of something rather quickly so he will shut the hell up and get me home. All I want is to crawl into my bed and pray like hell he leaves me alone.

"Oh, just how it was such a nice weekend. The thought of going back to work tomorrow doesn't sound so appealing."

"Take the day off, then. God knows you deserve it after working your ass off while I was gone."

Trent, you couldn't have come up with a better idea, I think to myself. Perfect excuse for me as I turn in my seat to face him.

"Are you sure you wouldn't mind?" I ask, turning on the charm.

"No. Not at all. Stay home and relax all day, or go have a shopping day. You know I don't care what you do."

Yeah, right, dipshit.

"Actually, I think I might call your mom when we get home and see if she wants to go shopping. I haven't talked to her all week."

I keep my eyes on his face to see his reaction but there is none, just an unfeeling, straight-ahead stare.

"That's a great idea. I need to call her myself. We have been so busy at work this past week that I didn't even give a thought to calling her."

All kinds of alarms start to go off in my head at his statement. Shit! I don't trust him or his mother to be together right now. When I make my not-so-pleasant visit to my dear old mother-in-law tomorrow, that will be one of the first things I demand of her. Stay the fuck away from Trent.

Weaving our way through traffic, the rest of the ride is nothing more than small talk regarding clients and audits and things from work.

Shit, we have access to so many people's personal information. Drowning in my own personal hell, I never even gave the business a thought at all this week. What the hell do I do about that? He obviously has to know something about accounting with the way he has talked and handled several clients on the phone this week.

Somehow I need to find a way to see exactly what it is he is doing in that office. I wonder what kind of damage he has done to the business Turner and I have worked so hard to create. Who the hell knows how many clients' books he could have screwed up, or if he is stealing from them?

I just have to shove all this work stuff aside for now and focus on the fact that my husband is missing and pray to God when this does get out people will understand. I am being pulled in so many directions I don't even know what is right or wrong anymore.

"I need to get some gas. Do you need anything?" Trent asks sweetly, sounding exactly like his brother.

"No. I'm good. Thanks."

I smile smugly into the darkness. Good. I need to make a phone call while you're inside paying for the gas.

He smiles as he pulls into the gas station and steps out of the car. The side mirror gives me a good view of him as he opens the gas cap and starts to pump the gas with his head facing away from me. Frantically I scrounge through my purse and find my phone, dialing Melody's number while keeping my eyes on Trent's reflection.

"Clove?" she answers, her voice sounding panicky.

"Melody. I don't have much time to talk. I just wanted you to know that I will be over to your house tomorrow morning at nine and I want answers."

"W-what do you mean? I told your brother everything that I know."

"Cut the bullshit. You and I both know there is more to all of this than you told Zack. I have a right to know everything and you're damn well going to tell me."

I hang up abruptly, not wanting her to say any more or try and weasel her way out of this. I drop my phone back into my purse and place it back on the floor of the car. As soon as I sit back up, Trent finishes and makes his way into the station.

Just as he gets inside, I hear an unfamiliar ping. I turn away from the window and look around for the source. It's his phone, which he placed in the cup holder between the seats. Making sure he is still inside, I grab the phone. For an imposter, he sure is dumb as hell . . . when I swipe the screen, he doesn't have it locked.

"Oh my God. No!"

I see who the message is from and tears form in my eyes as I gasp and place my hand over my mouth. The text is a picture of Turner lying on what appears to be a dirty mattress, bloody and bruised everywhere.

"Oh my God, Turner. What have they done to you?"

I softly rub my hands over the photo on the screen and silently curse any and everyone who has done this to my husband. I have no clue what makes me think so rapidly, but I reach down and dig my phone out, quickly taking a picture of my husband and setting the phone back in place.

My heart cannot bear looking at what they, he, or whoever has done, so I shut my phone completely off and keep it in the palm of my hand as I lay my head back on the headrest. Even though I want to cry, somewhere deep down I find the strength to hold it all in. Even when Trent climbs back in the car and takes off driving with his hand resting on my leg, I hold it in. I hold it in until we get home and I climb in my bathtub. Then, and only then, do I let my tears fall, all the while gripping my phone. It's the closest thing I have to him right now and yet I still can't bring myself to look at it again.

With unstable hands I power my phone back to life, all the while not even looking at the screen. It takes me several minutes before I am able to flip my phone over, and when I bring up the pictures and see Turner's battered and tortured form lying there, it's the most heart-rending thing I have ever seen. My entire body shakes thinking of what he has endured at the hands of his father, a man who doesn't even deserve the honor to be called that. And why?

I can't look at this anymore, so I hurry up and shoot a text to my brother explaining everything. Immediately he responds, asking me if I am going to be all right. My ever-overprotective big brother is undeniably doing his best to look out for me. He has attacked this with the wrath of a thousand suns and he's damn good at his job, one of the best on his force.

The pain he has to be going through tears me up inside. For all the issues and arguments Zack and I had growing up, not once have we not had each other's backs.

But this? No one should have to try and protect someone from what I am going through right now. It doesn't matter, anyway. Whatever happens, I really believe none of us are ever going to be okay again.

"Clove, you alive in there?"

I jump and almost drop my phone into the tub when Trent speaks from right outside the bathroom door.

"Yeah! I started to doze, is all."

I'm thankful as all hell my voice stays strong and doesn't show any of my hurt or anger.

"I did too, on the couch. Come on and let's go to bed."

Sleep isn't going to come to me at all tonight, and I know this. I let out the plug and with sluggish moves, I dry myself off and lotion up before brushing my teeth. When I pull Turner's t-shirt over my head and inhale his scent, I have to brace myself against the vanity for a moment before climbing into bed with the piece of shit stranger who had a part in the beating of my husband. I roll as far away from Trent as possible. He might want to sleep with one eye open tonight, because the way I feel right now, I may just stab him in his cold, black heart.

"You sure you can handle working by yourself tomorrow?" I ask more out of concern about what he will do when I am not there than anything else.

He chuckles, giving me the same damn sexy crooked smile I'm used to seeing on my husband's face, then stretches his naked torso around to turn off the light.

"I'm sure, babe. I'm fully trained to handle things on my own. I do have a degree just like you, you know." He moves a little closer so his hand rests on my hip.

A degree in kidnapping and how to fucking ruin people's lives, is more like it!

"I know you do. It's just that last week was so damn hectic, and I feel bad."

"Don't worry about it. Just have a good time with my mom and enjoy yourself, babe."

I know he wants me out of our office so he can do whatever the hell he does without any interruptions, but I let it go.

Trent tugs on my shirt to try and bring me a little closer to him. Rolling myself over so my back is to his front, I let him rub my hip. I squeeze my eyes shut but he doesn't move them any farther north or south. When his hand stills on my hip and I hear his breathing start to even out, I lay as still as I possibly can until I know he is sound asleep.

Ever so slowly, I lift his hand off of me and slide over to the other side of the bed. He rolls a little, but doesn't wake up. I can finally breathe as I lay there in the dark and stare through the window into the black, moonless night. I wonder if Turner is sleeping peacefully or if he is looking at the same dark sky as I am.

The stars are nonexistent tonight as they hide behind gray clouds. The dark doom of the night does nothing for my mood; if anything, it depresses me even more. Somehow my mind finds a way to shut down and my eyes drift closed, but even as I fall into a fitful sleep, something tells me that when I wake up I am not going to like this new day at all.

Chapter Thirteen

I must be dreaming, and it's such a good dream. I'm being cradled in my husband's arms as I feel his thick, hard erection running up and down the crack of my ass. I hear his sweet words of devotion and adoration as his hand comes around and firmly cups my breast while my ass presses into his cock.

And then I manage to push myself to the surface of reality. This isn't a dream, and it's not Turner who is up against me. It's Trent. He is moaning and grinding into my ass. His hands run over it, fondling and caressing it with the light touch of a feather. He slips my panties to the side and slides his finger up and down my crack. I feel my body responding as his finger starts to rim the edges of my puckered entrance. My eyes spring open and before I know it, he has me flipped over and lying flat on my stomach.

"What are you doing?" I squeak.

"I woke up with my dick so fucking hard from the best dream I have had in a long time."

I'm still slightly groggy from sleep so I inhale deeply, swallowing the burning feeling in my throat and forcing my mind to catch up and comprehend his intentions. I can only imagine what this dream has to do with. All of a sudden, it hits me. Oh, shit! Trent wants to fuck me in the ass!

It's as if he wants to control and stake claim to every part of my body. I cannot allow this to happen. I won't. I can't.

"Turner, stop," I demand.

I pull away from him so we are face to face.

"I don't want to stop, Clove."

He gently skates his free hand all the way up the side of my stomach and over my breast, and with one finger, trails up the center of my chest until he reaches my chin. He cups it for just a few moments.

Moving over to my cheek, his smooth hands stroke tenderly.

The room is eerily quiet as he continues to stroke my cheek. If I didn't know who this man was, I would think he truly cared by the way his touch is making me feel. It's a loving and caring touch, touches to calm me and soothe me, to convince me to let him do this. This is something I have never done before, and if I did, I would want it to be with the man I love.

I am scared out of my ever-loving mind to have this man touch me in one of my most intimate places. I close my eyes and again bring Turner's face into my mind, but the fucked up, twisted thing about picturing Turner's face is that I am also seeing Trent. Fuck me!

Can I conjure up enough strength to do this? It's all a part of the long road to get to the eye of this shit storm I am living in. Anything and everything I have to endure and go through is all for one simple word. Love. I love my husband and I need him back. I need to know he is safe and alive, even though every part of my ruptured and bleeding heart will be smashed into a million pieces, never to be put back together again.

"Are you with me baby? You're quiet and shaking."

In different circumstances the lightness in his voice would make me feel more at ease with this, save for the fact these circumstances have been brought on by his actions. Nothing he says or does will make this any easier on myself.

"I'm just scared, Turner. This is something we have never done before. Is this what your dream was about?"

I tilt my head to side even though he cannot see me.

"Yes it was. I woke up with this massive hard on wanting so badly to finish what we started in my dream. For me to claim your sweet, round ass. For me to claim every part of you, Clove. I need this. Together we can make this feel so fucking good for the two of us."

Fuck, that is what this is all about. He wants to claim me and mark me in a spot where Turner has never been. He's a sick fuck who scares the living hell out of me. What if I say no? What will he do?

I lie here in the dark with my enemy with my emotions going back and forth. I'm as twisted and fucked up as he is. Do I believe he won't make me do anything I don't want to do? Yes. I believe it. Not because he seriously doesn't want to. The reason is simple. Whatever plan he has been working hard at isn't complete yet and just like me he has to do everything he can to keep his game heading in the right direction.

This man can fuck, and he fucks well. Sex isn't a game, though, and neither is fucking someone in her most intimate place. Oh, God, please forgive me for the way I am thinking right now. How can I hate someone so much, and yet the mere thought of him fucking me sends a thrill spiraling through my body which arrows straight to my throbbing pussy.

Consequences be damned. I want this. Whatever carnal drug he has slipped into my warped brain has me willing to burn in the fiery depths of hell just to experience the pleasure I know awaits me. My core clenches and my ass begs for his touch.

Clove Calloway no longer exists in this moment. She has been replaced by a woman I don't recognize. Two minutes ago, that other Clove was scared to death of the thought of this stranger touching her there, wishing and hoping it was her husband instead. But now, the thought of what is coming, of him doing something to me that no one has ever done before, has me dripping wet.

I spread my legs and lie back on the bed, hearing him gasp as soon as my head hits the pillow.

"Is this a yes?" he asks with hushed excitement.

"Yes."

His hands trail down the back of my leg until they hit the curve of my ass. Without any warning, he grabs my panties and rips them off my body, making me shudder.

"Fuck, Clove. Do you have any idea how good this is going to feel for both of us? I promise to make it so good for you, babe. You will be begging me to fuck this sweet, tight ass of yours every chance we get once we're done."

His hands graze across my pussy as he slides one finger in and with precision starts to stroke me until I am lifting my ass up and pressing myself as far as I can go onto his hand.

"You are so damn responsive. I love that about you, Clove."

Out of the blue he stops his assault on my core, moving his hand to my rosebud and coating the outside with my wetness. He repeats this action several times teasingly as he dips his finger into me and then back out again, lubricating the rim of my ass until unexpectedly I feel the tip of his finger dip inside my dark hole. My first instinct is to push his finger right back out. I pinch my eyes shut trying to overcome this intrusion as he sinks his finger in further and further.

"Jesus Fucking Christ! You are going to grip my cock so hard with this tight hole and squeeze the ever-loving hell out of me. Hang with me, Clove. I just need to help loosen you up and get you nice and wet so I can get in there. Flip over for me."

Trent helps guide me over onto my stomach.

"Are you okay?" he asks as he hovers behind me and pulls me up onto my hands and knees.

"I'm more than okay."

And I am. My pussy is pulsing with a wave of warmth emanating from somewhere deep within and my ass is constricting and clenching as if it knows what is in store for it.

I hear Trent do away with his clothes then the bed dips behind me and he pulls me back up against him. I swallow nervously when I hear the snap of a cap being opened. My back is facing him, but when I turn to see what it is, he places the palm of his hand on the middle of my back as if to halt me.

"W-what is that?"

Nerves that were not there just a few minutes ago have surfaced making me hyper aware of what I am about to do.

"It's lube. I bought at the store the other day. I've always wanted to try it."

The first glimmers of daylight are dawning through the window. This time I do turn all the way around to see what he is doing. I choke back a gasp as my eyes land on Trent's rock hard cock, which is in his hand as he strokes himself up and down, applying the lube.

Jesus Christ! I am turned on like never before as he continues to fondle his large dick. Juices begin to seep out of my core and onto my leg at the sight.

Our gazes connect and for a fleeting moment I swear that I see the same look in his eyes as Turner always had whenever we made love. No, it can't be. It has to be my fucked up mind playing even more damn tricks on me. There is no way in hell this man has one ounce of care for me.

This man wants what he wants, and common sense tells me to get the hell off of this bed and run, but I won't. I have turned into a selfish human being as I watch him lower himself over me until his front is against my back. His mouth devours mine and his hand reaches around and pinches my nipple, causing my ass to push itself into him of its own accord. My greedy body betrays my mind as I prepare for the rawest, most primal fuck of my life.

"I've been thinking long and hard about what I am going to do to you, Clove. Been yearning for this sweet ass every motherfucking day. The way it sways back and forth when you walk. Whenever you bend over in front of me. It's mine. No one else's but mine. I am going to make you scream as I watch your cum drip all over these sheets."

I jolt at his words of seduction. My faculty of speech is gone as every part of my body starts to throb with want and need.

"Let me have your mouth, Clove. My tongue needs to fuck yours and there isn't a flavor of your body I don't crave."

He doesn't give me time to react, he just takes what he wants and drives his tongue into my mouth, kissing me so wild and passionately that I feel a hot summer storm brewing under my skin. Sweat begins to drip from my pores as he tweaks my nipple one last time, hard enough to inflict both pleasure and pain.

His hands graze slowly down my sides until the palms of his hands grip my ass firmly. We break our kiss, both of us moaning and panting heavily. Not wanting to wait any longer for him to fuck me, I claw at the sheets as I lay my head down on the pillow and lift my ass higher in the air.

"Fucking Christ, the light is perfect. I can see your dripping pussy and your ass is begging to be fucked right now, isn't it?"

My mind is so muddled it takes me a moment to decipher his question and when he spanks my ass, I yelp.

"Answer me. You want my cock to fuck this tight ass, don't you baby?"

Jesus, his words and the sting from his slap have me about to come already. I don't hesitate any longer in answering him. I practically scream my head off from the sexual frustration my body is experiencing.

"Yes. Fucking hell, yes! I want you to fuck me."

His finger penetrates my entrance slowly as he moves in and out of my ass, coaxing it more with my juices. The pressure on my nerve endings has me spinning into unknown bliss and when he pushes in further I cannot help myself. I bring my hand to my clit and apply pressure in small circles. Trent's finger hits an unfamiliar spot, which along with me rubbing my nub, sends me over the edge as I violently shake through an orgasm that hits me like a Mack truck.

"Fuck, yeah! Ride it out. Give it all to me. All of it," he begs as he removes his finger and places the tip of his cock at my hole. I'm still coming down from the high of my first orgasm when I feel him push in only a small part of the tip. My eyes pop open and I cringe from the pain. His cock is so much bigger than his finger, and oh, God. It hurts. I pull myself away from him slightly.

"Are you still okay?"

"Yes, I'm fine. Let's just go slow."

"Fuck me, baby. You are so tight. Damn, this feels amazing. The way you're squeezing my cock makes me want to come right the fuck now."

He plunges in deeper and a loud moan involuntarily escapes my lips. I should feel like this is an intrusion into this orifice. This is something I have rarely thought of doing before now, and even though I feel like I am being ripped wide open as he sinks his large cock all the way in, the pain gives way to exquisite satisfaction.

I have no control of the whimpers fleeing from my mouth as he starts to slowly move. The feeling is delicious as hell. I have never experienced anything like this in my life. I need more as he starts to fuck me harder and faster. I want to scream at the top of my lungs.

He's balls deep now and slamming away, the dirty words he's throwing my way turning me the hell on. My hand reaches for my own pussy and I am on the edge of control when I shove two fingers inside.

"Fucking hell, Clove. Oh! Fuck me, baby! I can feel your fingers as my cock fucks you. Jesus . . . please tell me this feels good to you, Clove. Please."

I know letting myself be taken this way is all kinds of wrong and yet his rhythm has me shoving my ass as far into him as I can go. He pulls out and slams into me even harder and I scream so loud I'm sure the neighbors hear me. I'm so far gone I don't even care.

"I need to hear you say it, Clove. Tell me how good this feels. Tell me you have wanted me to fuck you so rough. It's all for you. I want to do it all for you."

He's begging as if he really does care if I feel good or not. I can't think about what that means right now. All I want is for him to make me come again.

"Harder!" I shout, stroking my fingers wildly in and out of me as he does indeed fuck me with all his might.

I am writhing like an animal. It hurts like hell. It feels better than being fucked in my pussy any day of the week. It definitely feels wrong to love this and I don't fucking care.

"I am going to come, Turner! Oh, God! I am going to come NOW!"

My body lurches forward and I land face first onto my pillow, which muffles my strangled screams as an earth-shattering orgasm rips through my body. Trent keeps pumping my ass with his cock and it takes mere seconds before I feel another one building even stronger than before. He slams into me one last time, yelling my name in a strangled voice.

As I feel his hot come shooting inside me, I lift my hips and detonate right along with him.

Chapter Fourteen

I don't know how long we lie there trying to catch our breath and regain our composure. I don't even remember him pulling out or cradling me in his arms. What I do remember is the act I just let my so-called captor perform on me. The worst guilt I have experienced since this fucked up man entered my life hits me.

I brought this upon myself. I deserve to carry it and have it weigh me down for the rest of my miserable life. I deserve it. I welcome it, and I crave the guilt. Rolling over onto my back, one silent tear rolls down my cheek. How pathetic is that? Just one tear. Am I all cried out? Who the fuck knows anymore? One thing I do know is I will never be the same person I was before.

When my mind clears, I hear the shower running. Suddenly it turns off and I hear the squeak of the shower door opening. I listen to the noises of Trent moving around in the bathroom as he opens and closes a few drawers and then starts up an electric razor.

I pull the comforter over my hand to try and drown out the sound of him using my husband's personal things. He is wearing Turner's clothes, using his toothbrush. It's sickening and maddening all at the same time. I just want to curl up in a tight ball and cry and scream and lash out thinking about every aspect of this.

Once the razor shuts off and he is silent for a few moments, I pull the comforter back down and close my eyes, pretending to still be asleep. I hear the door open when he enters the bedroom. He rustles around in the closet for a bit and then I hear him at Turner's dresser opening a drawer and then closing it again.

The end of the bed dips as he sits and that is when I open my eyes and stare at the back of his head, watching him put on socks and shoes. Visions of me crawling up behind him and stabbing him right in his fucking back have me smirking.

God, I have never thought about killing anyone before in my life! Yet I welcome the thought of actually doing it more and more these days as my face twists into its now perpetual scowl. Yeah, if looks could really kill he would be so dead right now.

"Have a great day," my chirpy voice startles him.

"Shit, babe! You scared me. Sorry if I woke you."

He stands and comes around to my side of the bed.

"Oh, I need to get up anyway and get ready to go see your mom."

His jaw tightens and his lips twitch slightly as I study his reaction. He regains his composure as he bends down and kisses me on top of my head. He's singing a different tune than he was a few hours ago when he had his dick up my . . . God!

"Don't forget to tell her I said I will give her a call very soon." He grins and steps away.

"I'll make a pot of coffee and grab a bagel or something and leave you to your day then."

"See you for dinner then," I holler after him as he walks out the bedroom door.

Damn, I hope today I get the answers I need to lead me closer to finding Turner so I don't have to sleep another night in the same bed as this man.

I wait about fifteen minutes or so to make sure he is gone and then I hurl myself out of bed and rush into the bathroom. I take the quickest shower known to mankind, paying extra attention to my backside.

I feel sick to my stomach for enjoying myself. I need to keep reminding myself that it wasn't me who allowed him to do what we did. It wasn't me.

I am pretending to be someone I am not, just like he is. If I don't keep telling myself that over and over again, I am not going to survive this and I will never find Turner, ever.

Picking up my towel and haphazardly drying off, I rush around the bedroom. I am going for comfort today, putting on a pair of denim capris and a pale yellow tank top.

I stand in front of the mirror and braid my long hair off to the side. I waste no time brushing my teeth and applying minimal makeup. Finally, I slip into my black flip-flops and race downstairs to the kitchen.

I dump the remaining coffee out of the pot, afraid to even drink it. It could be poisoned for all I know. After seeing the picture of Turner and what this man has done to his own brother, who knows what the hell he would do to me? The man has no conscience at all and there is no way I trust him.

I shoot a quick text off to Melody letting her know I am on my way, then I grab my purse. I am out the door and on the road within thirty minutes of climbing out of bed. Setting my phone to hands-free, I hit my brother's number and he answers right away.

"Thank Christ you're all right, Clove. I have been worried out of my fucking mind all damn night."

I hear a hint of uneasiness in his tone. My nerves suddenly jump all over the place.

"What? Why?"

"My sister is living with a damn criminal, that's why. Shit, Clove! If he had any hand in what happened to his brother, what makes us think he wouldn't do the same thing to you, or worse? It's time you get out of there and come and stay with us."

"Are you serious, Zack? I am not leaving there. What if they kill him? Neither one of us would be able to forgive ourselves."

I can't even wrap my mind around the fact my husband could die over this. Dread so deep fills my mind and my body that I start to cry.

"Clove, listen to me. They want something and they are not going to kill him until they get it. Now I am not taking no for an answer. You are coming here and I fucking mean it. Do not go back to your house. You're my sister and I need you to be safe while we investigate this. I should have never let you go back with him in the first place, even though I have Martinez following you."

His voice sounds a little calmer at the mention of his partner's name. I look in my rear view mirror and yup, there is Martinez in his black SUV following a few cars behind me. My tears continue to fall and I let them, not giving a shit what I look like anymore.

I drive in silence as I listen to my brother's instructions. As soon as I am done talking to Melody, I am supposed to go straight to his house. Anxiety and panic set in and I start to shake. Can I do it? Can I live with myself knowing I could be risking my husband's life?

"Fine. Zack. I will be there, but I do have to stop at the house. I have absolutely nothing with me. Besides, Trent is at the office all day and like you said, Martinez is following me. I will run in and grab what I need and be back out within fifteen minutes," I promise, the tone of my voice letting him know I am not negotiating this with him.

"You'd better be here by noon, Clove, or so help me God I will come and get you myself," he demands.

"All right, all right."

"And stop crying, sis. You're going to get the answers we need from Melody, I just know you are, and it's going to put us even closer to finding out where Turner is."

I take a deep breath and listen to my brother try to calm me as I pull into Melody's drive. Martinez parks across the street.

Climbing out of my car and nodding in his direction, I move with purpose. Fuck me if I don't look up and Melody is standing on the front porch looking worse than I know I do.

Melody has betrayed both Turner and myself and as I transfix my gaze on her, she recoils as if I have just bitch slapped her . . . which is exactly what I will do if she doesn't give me one hell of a damn good reason as to why she has never told her son the truth all these years.

I continue to stay distant and cold as ice as I approach her.

"Good morning, Clove."

Her voice is unsteady and unsure.

"No. I wouldn't call it a good morning at all, Melody. Would you?"

I glare murderously.

"No, I guess it's not. And most likely never will be again, by the look on your face."

I say nothing as I pass her by and open the door to her house. She follows right behind me, and when I enter the foyer of her home my throat instantly goes dry when I see all the familiar pictures on the wall and fireplace mantle of Turner and myself. My eyes land on one of them and at lightning speed my legs have me standing in front of it.

"That photo has always been my favorite of the two of you."

"Yes. Mine too."

I feel her stand close behind me. I continue my survey and precious memories flood my mind of the day this picture was taken. Turner and I were so young and carefree then. It was taken by his mother about three months after we started dating.

We didn't even know she had taken it. Turner is sitting on a swing in the park as I sit on his lap with my legs straddling him. We are front to front as my legs hang loosely behind his back. His big, strong hands are cradling my face and our foreheads are touching. I loved him then and I love him now more than I ever thought possible.

"I know I have a lot of explaining to do. Most likely neither you nor my son will ever forgive me for keeping all of this from you, but please listen to everything I have to say, Clove."

I know Melody well, at least I thought I did, and she sounds sincere. I set the photo back down on top of the mantle and without even acknowledging her, I turn and take the few steps over to the loveseat in the corner of her spacious living room.

"I'll listen," I say as I sit down.

"Would you like something to drink?" she asks.

"No. What I want is for you to talk and tell me the truth so I can find my husband."

My voice is cold and full of hate. I don't give a shit anymore.

"You act as if I don't care about Turner's well being at all, Clove. He's my son, for God's sake."

"I know you love your son, Melody, and so do I. You're hiding something, damn it, and if it's something that can help us find him then don't you think you should speak up? I just don't under-"

She cuts me off by holding up her hand as if to silence me.

"You what? You don't understand? No one will ever understand the hell I have been through for twenty-six years. They're my children. Trust me when I say I know where my loyalties lie, but if you think this is easy for me well then you really don't know me at all, Clove."

I swallow back my pride and sit there waiting as she takes a seat across from me in a dark green wingback chair. She exhales loudly as she lifts her head to meet my gaze.

"I knew the day that James took Trent I would most likely never see my son again."

Tears well up in her eyes and she looks away from me.

"He was so abusive, Clove. I thanked God every day that my sons were too young to remember some of the horrible things their father did. And I will never forgive myself for the way he treated Turner."

"Zack told me all about it, but I am not here to listen to you tell me how you have suffered and will never forgive yourself. That is your guilt to bear, not mine. I need you to tell me why you never told your son the truth about having a brother- an identical twin at that. How could you keep something like that from him?"

Venom is spewing from my mouth at this point. I don't give a shit about the damage I may cause with my words.

"You sit over there and judge me all you want to, Clove, but you have no idea what kind of man James is and the things he could do and would do."

"Are you hearing yourself right now, Melody? Everything you have said to me so far is a bunch of shit."

Melody straightens her posture and looks me dead in the eye.

"He threatened to kill Turner," she says, her voice just a hint above a whisper.

"He *what*?"

"I reported my son missing the minute I knew he was gone. For months and months they searched for both of them. It was as if they just vanished. Trent was too young to go to school, so there were no school records. I have no clue how they survived or what they did. There was nothing, absolutely nothing anywhere. After about six months or so I received a late night visitor just as I climbed into bed."

Her eyes show the worst kind of pain I have ever seen and her body language suddenly goes stiff with what I assume are unpleasant memories entering her mind. I am a being a bitch and I know this, so I keep quiet to give her the time and space she needs.

"James was in my bed, waiting for me. I was dead tired that night from working and then coming home to a crying toddler. Turner cried for his brother for almost a year. My heart broke every time. What do you say to a little boy when you know his brother is never coming back?"

We stare at each other in silence and my heart cracks right down the middle, thinking of what Turner had to go through at such a young age.

"James put his hand over my mouth and told me he would kill Turner if I said even one word to him. I had never feared for anything in my life like I did that night. He hated Turner. His own flesh and blood."

I can't hold back the tears anymore so I just let them fall as I listen to her pained voice.

"H-he said Trent was dead, Clove."

I don't blink or turn my head away as I process what she just said.

"So you see? I never once gave up, because for all these years I thought my son was dead; dead at the hands of his own father. There was no way in hell I was going to tell Turner anything. As he grew up I was always afraid he would ask about Trent, but he never did. Not one time did he ask about his brother or his father. At the time I was grateful he forgot about them, but maybe he never did. I don't know. Maybe as he grew to understand things he didn't want to hurt me by asking. And now . . ."

She looks down at her hands, which are resting on her lap as she clasps them even tighter.

"Now I have a son who I love more than life itself, and another son who for all these years I have thought was dead and he's not. So yes, I am living through hell right now, and yes, I deserve to be there. I have to live the rest of my life with guilt and shame because I believed that animal, and now it appears that Trent is exactly like him. And . . ."

"And what?"

I know why he's here. I know exactly what they want from Turner."

Her voice is very soft as she continues.

"Turner is about to become a very rich man, Clove."

Her voice cracks and is filled with agony. I lean forward in my seat, stunned.

"What did you just say?"

Her body stiffens and she stands up and starts pacing the floor.

"He will inherit twenty million dollars when he turns thirty."

My mouth drops open and I feel like I have just been kicked in the teeth by this sudden revelation.

"How? Why? I don't understand. Does Turner even know about this?"

"No. He doesn't know about this. He does know that my parents are very wealthy, but you know how Turner is. Money isn't important to him in the sense that he has to have millions of dollars to survive."

All I can do is shake my head in disbelief as Melody continues on.

"I planned on telling him soon to prepare both of you for when the time came. Now I may never see my son again, all because they want that money. James knew those boys would be set for the rest of their lives. All these years he must have been keeping tabs on us, my parents included. And now that both of them are gone and those boys are about to turn thirty, what better way to get your hands on millions of dollars than to switch one twin for the other?"

"Hold on. Why didn't you just tell Zack all of this in the first place? Do you know where they are? Where might James have taken Turner?"

I know I sound bitter and angry, and a part of me believes I have a right to. She knew. All along she knew and she never said a word. And yet the part of me who loves and cherishes this woman is here berating her when all these years she has thought one of her children was dead and she has carried this burden alone. I just cannot wrap my head around how she must be feeling. For the past few days I have been living in fear of what could happen to Turner since he's been taken, but my mother-in-law has been living with the same fear for over twenty years.

I lift myself up and extend my arms out to her. Neither one of us needs words right now; we need each other.

She doesn't hesitate as she gets up and throws herself right into my arms. Her shoulders sag in defeat and we cry. We both cry, soaking both of our shirts with tears. She sobs and shakes uncontrollably.

"I don't know what to do, Clove," she wails, pulling herself away from me but gripping onto my shoulders as if I am her lifeline. "I wasn't thinking clearly when I came to your house the other day. All I could think about was seeing my son. This is such a dreadful and unforgivable thing for me to say, but I just can't think of that man who is pretending to be Turner as my son . . . not in the way the real Turner is. Even so, dear God, I'm still his mother! I will never be able to forgive myself for thinking that way."

I can only stand there staring at the pain and regret in her bloodshot eyes.

"I- I don't know what to say to that, Melody."

"There is nothing to say. Now listen to me," she says, her attitude suddenly changing. "I have no idea where James is. I do know he is a very dangerous man and if he raised Trent to be anything like himself, then he is just as dangerous. I wouldn't be able to live with myself if anything happened to you. You need to leave that house, now."

Her grip on my upper arms becomes a little firmer.

"I know," I say meekly. "I talked to Zack on the way over here. I am going to stop by the house and grab a few things, then go to his house." Suddenly, I become aware that once Trent finds out I am gone, there is no telling what he will do. "You know what? You shouldn't be staying here by yourself, either. You're coming with me."

"Oh, no. I couldn't possibly co-"

"Bullshit. Go pack a bag, right now."

"You can hold baby Nolan," I tease, and try to smile. She seems to be thinking for a moment as her eyes dart all over the room.

"You're right," she sighs. "If you're sure they won't mind, then yes, I believe it's wise for me to stay there, too. I just have to get a few things in order."

I shoo her with my hand.

"You're family and Zack would kick my ass knowing I left you here once I tell him everything. Speaking of which, I should call him right now."

She removes her hand and I spin around and grab my purse and retrieve my phone.

"Clove?"

"Yeah?"

I love you so much, young lady."

And I know she does. I will always feel guilty for ever doubting her love for me or for Turner.

Chapter Fifteen

Zack and Krista are more than thrilled to have Melody stay with them as well. I knew they would be. What better place for us to stay than with a cop?

If I had even a piece of my heart left to break, hearing Melody tell me how she went most her life thinking one of her children was dead would do it. Time does not heal all wounds when it comes to the death of a child. God, the hell she must have gone through every single birthday and holiday and first day of school, and graduation. It's a feeling I cannot even begin to comprehend.

Numbness sits in the pit of my stomach as I drive back to my house to gather my things. Martinez took Melody over to Zack's house and I promised him I would call him the minute I got home and the minute I left my house.

I just don't understand how James could be so cold and calculating toward a child he helped create, and I probably never will. Over money? Money can be such a dirty word. It makes people do things they normally wouldn't do, like turn family members into victims. Is James going to make Trent a victim, too, or is Trent already just as ruthless as his father?

My phone rings and I see it's Zack, so I answer right away.

"What the hell do you think you are doing?" he screams in my ear.

"What are you talking about?" I scream back, frustrated.

"Jesus Christ, Clove! You didn't tell me you were going back to your house on your own. What the hell are you thinking? I told you! Fuck! Just get your shit and get the hell out of there."

"Zack, did something happen within the last half hour? You're scaring the shit out of me."

He lets out a long breath.

"Nothing has happened. I just . . . damn it. We found out that James spent four years in fucking prison for stabbing someone down in Tennessee."

"What the hell? And you're just telling me this now?"

"The information only came over a little while ago. The guy is a fucking loose cannon. And hell, from what you told me on the phone about him, I don't want you going anywhere by yourself. I think it's time we tell Dad about this, too."

The thought of telling my dad is enough to shatter that last chunk of my heart. He'll be worried sick, but now I know I cannot keep something like this from him any further.

"Give him a call and have him come over after work. We can all sit down and talk this out."

All I can see is the look on my dad's face when he finds out what's been going on. He always told me his love and support for the both us was unconditional. Ever since this nightmare started, all I have wanted was for him to give me one of his big, strong hugs and tell me everything is going to be all right.

"Listen, get your shit and get the hell out of there. There should be an unmarked car with a couple cops parked across your street right now. And, Clove?"

"Yeah?" I sigh as I turn into my drive and see the unmarked car across the street.

"Love you, sis."

"Love you too, Zack. Tell Krista I will be over there in about a half hour."

"You'd better be, damn it."

"I will be. Now let me go so I can get there."

"I am walking out the station door as we speak and then I will tell you everything we know."

"Sounds good. See you in a bit."

I hang up the phone and toss it on the seat so I can hit the garage door opener. Pulling my car inside, I wave to the two cops sitting in the car directly across the street. God, I hope we're doing the right thing here.

As I enter my home I am startled at the scene I see in front of me. Someone has turned it upside down. Everything is scattered all over the floor. The drawers are all pulled out and thrown all over the floor- papers, silverware, everything. I am rooted to the spot and I am scared to even take one more step for fear whoever did this is still here.

Turning back around, I reach for the door handle to get the hell out of there when I am grabbed from behind and a hand is firmly clamped over my mouth.

"Hello, Clove." The voice I desperately never wanted to hear again whispers in my ear.

Fear and panic set in and I struggle to get out of his hold as Trent grabs me securely around my waist. Between the hand covering my nose and mouth and the intense pressure he is applying to my stomach, it's difficult for me to breathe. I kick and claw at his arms and legs, digging my nails into the flesh of the arm that is gagging me. He hisses in pain as I continue to tear at him ruthlessly.

"Fucking bitch!" he shouts.

I can't shake him. I feel lightheaded and my breathing gradually becomes shallower as he squeezes the life out of me. He's going to kill me. I am going to die right here in my own home. I see my entire life fading away as my life flashes before my eyes.

Every good memory I have ever had will be gone in a matter of minutes. My dad comforting me with words of encouragement after falling off my bike as a young child. My graduation. My wedding day . . . oh God, my wedding day.

I can't hold back the tears any more when I think about that day. The day I married my best friend. How can I forget the look on his face when I approached him at the altar? Turner looked at me as if I were the most beautiful thing he had ever seen, and he told me as much.

I was all dressed and ready to leave for the church, so I gathered my things and went to slip my feet into my white pumps. That's when I noticed the little love poem Turner wrote on the bottom of my shoe. I turned the shoe over in my hand and read his words in surprise.

'Today, you become my wife. This makes today the best day of my life.'

I don't want it to be over yet. No!

But there is nothing I can do as my eyes start to close of their own accord. My struggles cease immediately and my arms fall limply to my sides.

"I'm not ready for you to die yet. I've enjoyed fucking you too much, Clove."

He lets go of me completely and shoves me to the floor where I gasp and cough, trying to get as much air and oxygen as I can.

"Get up." His voice drips with malice.

"Go fuck yourself," I say, regaining my voice.

He remains quiet for what feels like an eternity and my breathing finally comes back to normal. His stillness begins to scare me, but I will not die without a fight. I will never give up until I breathe my last breath.

I brace myself up on all fours and try to lift myself up, but as I start to stand, he grips a giant handful of my hair and whips me around. I fall back to the floor, hard, my hands flying up as if to ward off the pain he is inflicting.

I scream when he starts to drag me across the floor. He stops and yanks me up to meet his face as he kneels in front of me. He's consumed with hatred. I can see it as plain as day seeping out of his eyes and boring into mine.

"Shut your motherfucking mouth. One phone call to my father and your fucking pussy of a husband is dead. This ain't no fucking joke, sweetheart, so do as I say and this will go a hell of a lot easier for you."

My head throbs as he violently jerks my hair back and I met his steely, cold eyes. I refuse to let him become aware of the fear his words have caused me. Instead, I make direct eye contact with him indicating I will not be an easy victim. He lifts his eyebrows as if to mock my stare and I spit directly in his face.

He releases his hold on my hair and even though I desperately want to cry, I reach deep inside and think of what Zack told me a few days ago. To hold onto love. What Turner and I have with each other will be all the strength I need to get me through this.

Wiping the spit from his face with the sleeve of his shirt he continues to stare at me.

"You know," he says with a slight ridicule in his words, "You're beautiful, smart, and one hell of a fuck, but I never pegged you for a woman with balls like a man."

At that, he brings up his hand and slaps me across my face so hard he sends my head reeling back. The pain of the sting causes adrenaline to course through my veins, and yet I still say nothing. Fuck him. He can beat me all he wants.

"You will pay for that, you dumb cunt. Let's get one thing straight, Clove."

He grabs hold of my chin and puts his face just a mere inch from mine.

"If you want to see my dear old brother ever again, then I suggest you listen to me and do exactly what I say. I am not fucking around with you anymore."

The muscles in his neck are twitching and his eyes look like they're about to pop out of his head. Good lord, this man is deranged.

"How can you hate your own brother so much? What did he ever do to you?" I whisper.

He just continues to stare at me as if I have struck a nerve. So many emotions reveal themselves in his eyes. I can see them all. Hurt, anger, pain. They're all there.

"He was fucking born. *That's* what my brother did to me. You may think you know everything, but trust me, you fucking don't. I am a hell of a lot smarter than you think I am, so whatever kind of shit you have brewing in that pretty little head of yours, I suggest you stop now. Because trust me, baby. IT. ISN'T. GOING. TO. WORK. My dear ole brother is as good as dead, bitch."

Oh God, no. It all hits me at once. It doesn't matter what I do or say, or if I help him get whatever it is he wants. They're going to kill Turner anyway.

"You take me to Turner first."

My voice never wavers or shows any sign that I am scared out of my ever-loving mind. Trent throws his head back and laughs in the most sinister way.

"That has to be the funniest damn thing I have ever heard. You see, Clove? I knew all along that you knew who I was, so don't try and play me for a fucking fool. You will get me what I need or I will call dear old dad. Or, better yet, I will take all kinds of pictures of you spread out nice and naked and ready for me to fuck, and send them to your precious Turner so that the last thing he will see before he dies is me fucking his wife."

"Good God! What kind of life did you live that you have so much hatred inside of you for a man who would have given anything to have a brother?"

"SHUT THE HELL UP. You know nothing about me or my life. As for my brother, I could give two fucks about him. You, on the other hand, are the best fucking piece of ass I have ever had. Trust me on this, babe. I am going to have you over and over again, whether it be right in front of my brother, or when I have you tied up and gagged. Either way I am going to get one more sweet taste of that creamy pussy of yours."

He rakes his eyes down my body until they land right at my core, making me feel naked and exposed.

"I am curious about one thing, though."

He lifts his brows with a shit-eating smirk on his face.

"Why did you let me fuck you when you knew exactly who I was?"

He tilts his head to the side with a look that says, *lie to me, bitch, and see what happens.*

"You know damned well why! It made me sick having you put your filthy hands on me. You repulse me."

His laugh echoes.

"That's not what this sexy body of yours said every time my cock was buried deep inside of you. You enjoyed every minute of it. I must say you have the sweetest tasting pussy I have ever had, and so responsive, too. I bet my brother doesn't fuck you like that, does he?"

He observes me, waiting on my answer unspeaking and motionless. I am not going to give him the satisfaction of letting him know anything more about Turner and me than I have to.

"You're fucking crazy," I sneer at him.

"Oh, baby I know I am. Don't you fucking forget it."

His words sting. They sting even worse than the blow I took. I need to think. I hope I can stall him. I'm praying like hell that when I don't show up at Zack's house within the half hour I promised and he doesn't hear from me, he will know something is wrong and be over here in minutes.

"How did you know I knew about you?" I ask, to keep him talking.

"You don't think I would come in here and pretend to be my brother without knowing everything about him and you, did you?"

"I want to know. How did you do it? Were you spying on us?"

He simply shrugs.

"It doesn't matter how I did it. What matters is I pulled it off, and you so graciously helped me without ever even knowing it. The thing is, this wasn't something we planned to do overnight. We have been waiting for this opportunity for years and living right under your nose. The best part of waiting all this time to become Turner Calloway was the look on my brother's face when he saw me. You should have been there to see our happy little reunion; it was priceless, I tell ya. Everything went according to plan. My brother fell right into our trap before he knew what hit him."

A malevolent laugh erupts from Trent. Every distasteful and wretched image of this ultimate betrayal imbeds itself in my mind. I jerk myself free of his grasp and I start savagely swinging and connecting with any part of his body I can find.

"You fucking prick!"

I am kicking and screaming and he takes it. He takes every swing and hit and scratch that I am throwing his way.

"I hate you, you sick fuck! Turner has never done a damn thing to hurt anyone. You're his brother, you fucking piece of shit!"

He just laughs, which fuels my fire even more. My arms and legs start to scream with pain with every connection I make to his body, and he just fucking laughs at me.

I pull back when my strength gives out on me and the tears finally start to fall.

"How could you?" I sob. "How could you do this to your own brother? Do you have any idea the hell that your mother has been through? Do you?"

"Ah, my mother. How is dear old mom, anyway? Never mind, don't answer that. You, Melody, and Turner will soon be together for one last little family reunion and I can ask her myself."

God he is so malicious and so full of hatred it makes me almost feel sorry for him. I start to laugh, and I mean laugh, as he has no clue where his mother is and he won't be able to get to her at my brother's house.

"What the hell is so funny?" he growls while right up in my face.

"You are. You think you're the only one who has done their 'homework?' Well, you may have, although it was pretty half-assed. But let me tell you something- you fucking failed the test, asshole. My brother had you pegged the minute he laid eyes on you. Your little plan is fucked. You and your father may think you're in the driver's seat of this preposterous game you're playing, but you're not."

He studies me closely as I lean in closer to him. His expression changes from shock to despair quicker than the beat of my racing heart.

"Yes, that's right, fuck face. Melody is gone. She knows everything. You will never get your revenge on her. She's gone and she's safe."

I look at him smugly.

"All this so-called *homework* you did is about ready to blow up in your fucking face. You may think you're the one calling the shots here, but newsflash, Trent. Any minute now my brother is going to come barreling through that door and trust me, you're going to regret every last one of the few short minutes he lets you live."

Chapter Sixteen

Without saying a damn word he analyzes my every feature to see if I am telling the truth. I am, and he knows it. His facial expression turns from that of a cold-hearted monster to a freaking animal as he grabs me by my throat and raises me up in the air, slamming my body into the wall.

"You stupid cunt! I will kill anyone who walks through that motherfucking door, including your pansy ass brother. No one will stand in the way of what is rightfully mine, even him."

He wrenches his hand away from my throat and I crumple to the floor, coughing and gagging, trying to catch my breath.

"Get the hell up, Clove. We're fucking leaving here, now."

His face contorts into a glare of pure hatred as he grabs my arm and yanks me up. I wince and cry out in pain as he drags me to the door.

"If you want to see Turner, you will do exactly as I say. I know you have a couple of cops sitting out there. I am going to slip into the backseat and you are going to drive. Do not do anything stupid. One phone call is all it will take and he will be dead. Do you understand what I am telling you?"

"I understand."

I will do exactly as he says as long as it gets me to Turner. With this in mind, I turn the knob on the door and enter the garage. He opens my car door and shoves me inside before lying down on the floor behind my seat.

"I will shoot you on the spot if you do anything at all. You wave at them and keep fucking driving, bitch. Don't you fucking speed or do a damn thing to get us pulled over until we get to where we need to be. Oh, and one more thing. Give me your phone."

His voice doesn't sound as distressed or troubled as it did before. He's calm, and for some reason I don't like calm Trent. What does he have planned? Where is he taking me?

"Phone, Clove. Now."

His hands come over the top of the seat and I reach down and hand it to him. He opens the car door and drops it on the ground.

"Now get us the hell out of here," he commands.

With trembling hands, I turn the key in the ignition and start the car. I see the unmarked cop car is still sitting there as I slowly back out into the driveway. Fuck, they're going to follow me since they think I am going to Zack's house. Shit, what do I do?

Acting as if nothing is wrong, I politely wave as I pull past them. My eyes keep flickering back and forth between the road ahead and my review mirror. When I see the cop car make a U-turn and start to follow me, panic starts to set in. My heart starts to beat loudly and feels like it is going to explode. When I turn the corner, they are just a few car lengths behind me. Shit. This is bad; I can sense it. I am going to have to try and outrun them, but first I know I have to make Trent aware of the situation and this is going to piss him off even more. Who knows what he will do if I don't, though?

"Where am I going?" My voice is a stuttering mess.

"Get on the highway and head south until I tell you to."

"Um, the cops are following us," I blurt out and chew on my bottom lip while I wait for his response.

"I figured they would. I got it all planned out. All you have to do is drive like you normally would and shut your damn mouth."

Fuck you! I want to scream back at him. I fantasize about getting on the highway and driving like a bat out of hell, and then ramming this fucker into the nearest pole, killing us both. That way neither one of us will get a damn thing out of this whole fucked-up situation.

It doesn't matter if I live or die right now, anyway. My life is over whether he kills me or I kill myself. Turner is never going to want me back after this, and even though I have said time and time again I would be able to live my life without him, I know I won't be able to. He *is* my life, and without him my existence is empty and meaningless. The only thing that matters to me right now is seeing him, even if it's for the last time.

I pull onto the expressway and travel the speed limit for a few miles in silence before Trent finally speaks.

"Get off on the exit to your brother's house and pull into the gas station on the right. You'll see a white truck parked on the left side. Pull up right next to it and then get out. I want you to go into the gas station and buy something, and then walk back out and get in that truck."

He really is fucking crazy. I could tell anyone in that store he has kidnapped me and he wouldn't even know. The wheels are turning big time in my head. If I play this out right and let the clerk know my situation, he could inform the cops who are behind us. Maybe somehow they can follow or track us. Think, Clove. You can do this. There has to be a way for them to be able to follow us without him picking up on it.

Trent must sense some of what is going through my head.

"Don't even think about telling anyone in that store a damn thing, bitch. If I think you peeped even one fucking word to anyone, your family will be burying you right next to your fucking husband."

I have never been so scared in my entire life. I hope like hell they at least let me see Turner so we can try to figure out a way out of this. I glance down at the clock and see it has been almost an hour since I hung up the phone with Zack. He has got to be freaking the hell out by now and has blown up my phone wondering where I am and why I am not answering. I am sure he has talked to the two officers who are still several cars behind me.

I turn on my blinker to indicate I am getting off on the exit, and when I look in my mirror I notice the cops are, too. They still have no idea Trent is in the car with me.

"How are you going to get out of the car without them noticing you? They're going to see you."

"Don't worry your beautiful little head about what I am going to do. You just do what you're told."

His hand reaches up over the top of the seat and grabs my hair as we come to a stop at the end of the exit. I cry out in pain and shock.

"Quit asking so many questions. Just do what you're fucking told, Clove."

He releases his hold on my hair as tears start to form in my eyes. I don't know how much more I can take. I feel like I am at my breaking point. I don't want to just sit by and do nothing, so when I pull into the gas station I decide I am going to say something to someone in there. The way things stand now it really doesn't matter what I do or don't do, because once they have gotten whatever they need out of Turner and me, they are going to kill us, regardless.

Wait. I remember Trent said he needed something from me when we were back at my house. Desperately I try to figure out what it is. If I am the only one who can get him what he needs, then maybe, just maybe, I can make some demands of my own.

Pulling up next to the truck, I put the car in park and shut it off. I gather my purse and just when I am reaching for the door handle to get out, Trent's brutal words halt my hand in midair.

"Wait one motherfucking second, bitch. There is something you need to hear first before you step out of this car."

He takes out his phone and dials a number. There is a slight pause before the line is picked up.

"Yeah, Dad, we're on our way. I told you she was a feisty one, but I know how much she loves that pussy of a brother of mine, so if you don't hear from me in five minutes, blow his fucking knee cap out."

His voice sounds vengeful, and yet why do I feel like I hear the smallest hint of regret when he speaks? Maybe it's just wishful thinking on my part. Not wanting to hear anymore, I jump out of the car and head into the back of the gas station where I grab a bottle of water and a bag of chips. I now know exactly what I am going to do to try and keep Turner alive.

There are two people standing in line in front of me at the checkout lane as I wait impatiently, constantly checking my watch. I have a minute and a half left to get this done. Sweat pops up on my forehead and I start tapping my foot. *Come on!* Thirty seconds remain when I finally drop my items onto the counter.

"Will that be all, miss?" The clerk behind the register asks.

For a few seconds I stare at her blankly, trying to decide what to do.

"Yes," I finally squeak out.

She immediately scans my items. I hand her over a five-dollar bill and grab my stuff and make my way to the door.

"Miss! Your change!" she calls out.

"Keep it."

I scramble through the door and scan the area looking for the cop car. When I see it parked on the opposite side from where I am, my nerves go on high alert. I round the corner of the gas station and open the passenger side door of the truck.

"Hurry the hell up." Trent leans over and jerks me roughly inside. "Scoot all the way down in the seat and stay there until I tell you to get up."

How I would love to deny him and tell him to shove his demands straight up his ass. But I do as I am told and slide down in the seat as he starts the truck and pulls out. He now has on a baseball cap and sunglasses, trying to hide his looks.

As long as I stay ducked down like this I am not going to have a clue where we are going, so I try and pay attention to the turns he is making. I realize he has turned back onto the highway heading in the direction we just came from. Trent looks repeatedly into the rear view mirror and I study his facial expressions, trying to figure out what he is thinking and if we're being followed. He seems completely at ease, as if he doesn't have a care in the world. He shows no signs of panic or worry. I wish he would take those damn sunglasses off so I could see his eyes.

My legs start to cramp up as I continue to sit on my hands and knees in the front of the truck. Fuck him and his damn demands. I cannot keep my mouth shut anymore.

"By the look on your face I would say the coast is clear, so I am getting up now." I put what little bit of strength I have left into my words.

"I don't think so."

He lifts an eyebrow and smirks down at me.

"Fuck you! I am not riding like this any longer," I insist, pulling myself up from the uncomfortable position I was in. Several minutes tick by before he speaks again.

"I should force you to kneel like that more often," he smirks. I whip my head around and glare at him.

"I will never kneel for you, you prick."

"Oh, but you will, Clove. Any time I tell you to kneel, you will."

"Like hell, I will."

"Well you see, Clove, one of the things I like about you is that gorgeous mouth of yours. I know firsthand what it can do, and baby, you do it so well. We have a hell of a long drive ahead of us and I am going to need some relief, so when I tell you to get on your hands and knees and suck my cock, you will."

I turn my head and look out the window, and as I tick off the miles one by one, I sink further and further into the abyss of self-hatred. Vivid memories of the things this man has done to me and the way my body reacted invade my mind. But not this time. If he even looks like he's trying to put his dick in my mouth, I won't hesitate to bite that fucking thing off.

Chapter Seventeen

We've been driving for nearly two hours now in complete silence. No radio, no nothing. We have crossed the Alabama state line and are headed west toward Mississippi. Trent said we have a long way to go. That could mean our destination is anywhere from Mississippi to California. I really don't know. All I know right now is I have a crook in my neck, my legs are killing me, I have to pee, and I am starving, but I refuse to ask this man for a damn thing.

It's obvious we were able to lose those two cops back at the gas station. I sure as hell feel sorry for them both right now as I know my brother has gone ballistic on them for losing me. My mind is churning with worry thinking about my dad, and Melody, and all of our friends. My father will come unglued at this news. My heart feels heavy and it suddenly feels too hot. I can hardly breathe, thinking of the pain my family is going through. Zack is a detective, for God's sake. He's going to think this is all his fault.

I close my eyes, imagining the look of sheer terror written across his face as he enters my house and sees everything all over the place. He loves me too much to try and pursue this case in a professional manner; it's personal now, and I feel sorry for anyone who tries to get in his way.

I flinch when I suddenly feel Trent's strong grip on my wrist.

"Are you all right over there? Jesus Christ, what are you mumbling under your breath about?"

Did I say all of that out loud? I yank my wrist out of his grip and turn my head away from him. I will not talk unless I absolutely have to.

"Don't act like a bitch, my love. Like I said, we have a few days and nights together, so when I ask you a question, you'd better fucking answer me. Now what the hell are you carrying on about over there?"

Shifting my body in my seat, I scrutinize his every feature, every move he makes as he drives. Even though you really can't tell them apart on the outside, there are so many differences between these two.

Oh, he did a mighty fine job disguising himself as Turner. For those few days until my brother discovered the truth, he had me fooled. Who knows how long I would have continued thinking Turner was cheating on me if my brother hadn't followed up on his gut instinct about this fucker's strange behavior?

That is what makes me feel guiltiest of all . . . that Zack sensed it and I didn't. How could I have been so blind? I knew the minute he touched me there was something different about my 'husband,' but I was too caught up in my arousal to think about it, turned on by the roughness of the way he took me.

I'm mortified and disgusted that I let my libido overrule my common sense. Even though it would have been nearly impossible to prove without the physical evidence of the fingerprints my brother ran, I still feel as if I somehow should have known as soon as I met him at the airport that this man was not my husband.

Trent senses my gaze on him and turns to smirk at me. Self-righteous bastard.

"I don't even have to ask if you like what you see when you look at me, Clove. I already know you do. I look just like him, don't I? Or should I say, he looks just like me, since I am actually five minutes older."

"Wipe that stupid grin off your face. You may look exactly like him, but you are nothing like him at all! You're nothing more than a sick, fucked up animal. You take advantage of people, and you use people, and you hurt people for no good reason. You make me fucking sick."

I pause to take a deep breath as this . . . this man gets under my skin.

"Ah, Clove. You are such a dramatic, uppity bitch with a mouth that I happen to like. If the circumstances were different I would be fucking that sassy ass mouth as much as I possibly could. As a matter of fact, I seem to recall you loving it when you took my cock in your mouth and I fucked your sweet pussy until you came all over me. Didn't think I was sick and fucked up then, now did you?"

He looks at me out of the corner of his eye with a sly smile.

"You can sit there and pretend all you want, Clove, but you knew it was me doing all of those delicious things to your body and not my brother, and you loved it anyway. You and I both know it. You have my scent all over you, baby doll. I marked you, and that will be something you will never be able to forget."

At that, he starts to laugh malevolently like the crazy motherfucker he is. I reach across and slap him as hard as I can. The truck swerves slightly but he gets it back under control at once. He growls and lunges for me with his free arm. I have nowhere to go when he grabs my arm and twists it until I scream in pain.

"You're fucking crazy, woman! You must have a death wish or something you foolish slut."

He twists even harder and I swear I hear something snap in my upper arm as my eyes well up in tears. I am speechless as he jerks me toward him and the seatbelt digs into my skin, causing it to burn across my chest.

"Let me tell you something, Clove. You will die when I say you will die, and not one second before. Now just for that stupid as fuck move you just made, I am done making threats. You are going to pay dearly for that. It's time you learn who is in control here, babe, and it sure as fuck ain't you. I am done having you test my patience and even more done with you thinking you can hit me. No one hits me. And I mean *ever*."

He shoves me away and my first instinct is to reach up and rub my arm. God it hurts, but I refuse to let the unwanted tears fall and for him to see both the physical and emotional pain he is inflicting on me. He is so much different from his brother in every way possible.

For one thing, no matter how mad Turner has ever gotten, he has never laid a finger on me and he never would. Turner would never call me names, either. Sure, we fight just like any other couple does, and our life is far from perfect, but it's ours and I want it back.

The possibility that I never will, has me wanting to land on death's doorstep as soon as I possibly can. I am not going to stop pushing Trent. I am going to push him until he snaps, and I know he will. I may be shortening my own life, but I don't give a shit.

"You don't scare me, you know?"

He raises an eyebrow at me.

"You need me for something, something you couldn't find at my house. You're shit out of luck there, Trent. You can't inflict any more pain on me than what you already have, so you can fuck off if you think I am going to help you get your hands on any of that money."

He doesn't say a word. Instead, he picks up the speed on the truck and pulls off onto the nearest exit. My heart starts to race. I am afraid that I have pushed him past his limit with my words.

He comes to a stop, and after looking both ways, he turns right and then makes a quick left into a carpool parking area. There are several cars parked but I see no one around as he pulls into the rear of the lot and slams the truck into park.

His whole demeanor changes as he reaches over and snaps open the glove box. When I see the long, shiny blade of a knife, I start to shake. He pulls it out and flicks the glove box closed, and without speaking opens his door and walks around the back of the truck. I jump in my seat as I see him heading toward my door.

Fuck, what is he going to do? I can see the expressway from here but it's too far away for anyone to see what is going on in the parking lot. Behind us stretches a deep patch of woods. Shit. Shit. *Shit!*

I try to stay calm as he swings open my door and then reaches across and unhooks my seat belt. He still hasn't said a word, which scares me even more. He stands there for several drawn out moments breathing way too heavily for my liking.

"Get the fuck out of the truck. Now!" he bellows and raises the knife to within an inch of my face.

I do as I am told. He drops the hand holding the knife to his side and grabs me around the waist, pulling me flush against his body. I flinch and try to wiggle free, but he's too strong. He takes my hands and holds them behind my back, and then walks us backwards until my body is up against the truck. I am shaking uncontrollably as I have no clue what is going through his mind or what he has planned.

"I told you to shut your fucking mouth and you didn't listen. Now you have pushed me just a little too far, Clove. This is not how I wanted things to go down between us, but you need to be taught a lesson. This is not a fucking joke!"

Oh, God. He has me cornered here like a small animal, and he is the predator. Is he going to kill me before I get the chance to see Turner? I do the only thing I can think of in a moment like this. I scream, and when I do, I instantly know that doing so was a huge mistake. In a blur of motion, Trent pulls back his fist and punches me in the stomach.

All the air is knocked out of me, and I feel vomit rising up in my mouth. He grabs me by the throat and walks us to the back of the truck. I can't move to protect myself . . . I can barely stand as my stomach twists and turns. The pain is almost more than I can bear. Opening the tailgate of the truck, he hoists me up and pushes me flat on my back.

"Who has the control here, Clove?" He grabs my face and wrenches it so I am staring into his face.

"WHO. HAS. CONTROL?" He raises his voice slightly.

I am sobbing uncontrollably at this point. I can't tune my mind out, it is spinning out of control as I gasp and wheeze as he towers over me.

"Oh, so now you have nothing to say, huh? No words, Clove? Am I scaring you? You *should* be scared, my darling. It didn't have to come to this, but you leave me no choice."

I am trying to shut him out of my consciousness, to close myself off from the fact that he is about to do God knows what, but I can't. All I see is him and the feral way he is looking at me.

"Please," I sniffle through my tears.

For the briefest of moments, I think he is going to relent. But then, he sits the knife down on the ground and reaches for something behind me. My eyes grow wide as I see his hand reappear in my vision holding a twisted braid of rope.

Immediately I start to thrash about and struggle to get away from him, but he won't have it. He pulls my hands over my head and climbs on top of me as he weaves the rope around my hands to secure them together.

I continue to kick and scream at him to get off of me until he slaps me in the face, extinguishing whatever will I may have had left in me to try and fight. I hurt everywhere. My stomach is clenching and a griping pain courses throughout my lower abdomen. My face is on fire and I can tell it is starting to swell. My arms ache as they are stretched tight above my head. I think the one he grabbed earlier is sprained.

"H-help," I croak weakly, but my throat is raw from screaming and the words don't make any sound.

"There isn't anyone here to help you, sweetheart."

Trent grinds his pelvis into mine and I feel how hard he is. Having me bound like this is turning him on. I feel my world tilt and slip from underneath me as I fully realize what is about to happen to me. My body convulses in fear.

"Oh, God! Trent, you don't want to do this! I beg you, don't. I know you're above this. I'm your brother's wife, for God's sake. Please!" I beg.

He looks into my tear stained face and he doesn't seem to care. This cannot be happening to me! Where is everyone? The way he has the truck parked, no one can see us without driving right by this spot.

As if he senses the direction of my thoughts, he shoves me even further back into the truck bed and climbs in, slamming the door behind himself. He gets on his knees at the other end and pulls out a roll of tape.

"God, don't do this, Trent. Don't!"

"I told you to shut your damn mouth, and now you will."

He rips off a piece of tape and places it across my mouth. I am defenseless and there is nothing I can do. I close my eyes as I feel him shift around.

"Open your fucking eyes and watch, Clove."

I open them wide and I see him hovering over me with the knife in his hand.

"On second thought, I don't think I need to use this since you can't move or talk."

Tilting his head to the side, he studies my features. I know he sees the fear in my eyes. How could he not? It's written all over my body.

He pushes the hem of my shirt up and licks his lips as he stares down at my exposed breasts, my chest heaving up and down.

"Fuck me. You have the best tits in the world. So ripe and pink and fucking ready for me to suck and fuck."

He firmly takes them in his hands and kneads them. When I cringe from his touch, he pinches my nipples so hard tears form in my eyes again. He's enjoying torturing me like this. All of a sudden, he grabs hold of the cups of my bra and rips them down, dropping his head to suck one of my nipples into his mouth. The pressure is so intense that I cry out through the tape in pain and start to shake.

Trent is in his own deranged world. He continues his onslaught until it seems as if he has gotten his fill. When he lifts his head and looks at me with hunger I know what's coming next. He unzips his pants and pulls his erection free. I can't look. I can't look. I turn my head away but he reaches up and yanks it back.

"Do not take your eyes off of me or I will fuck you up. You got it, Clove?"

I nod yes in shock and then I hear my panties being ripped off. Before I even know what is happening, he is on top of me.

I try to take my mind and body to the only happy place I have ever known . . . my husband's arms. But when I stare up into the eyes of my attacker my security is ripped away, because no matter how hard I try to think of Turner, all I can see is the man who is raping me.

He thrusts and thrusts, taking by force what is mine to give. His expression is contorted; his eyes have turned from green to black as if he is a man possessed. He is pounding into me so deeply I feel as if he is ripping me apart.

I feel him shudder with the force of his release as he comes inside me. I crawl into my own shell and scream from the agony of the pain being inflicted on my heart and body. My eyes are now clenched shut and he's not moving. I need him off of me. God, please get him off me!

"Clove? Jesus Christ, what have I done? Not to you, Clove. Oh, fuck me! No, no, no, not to you! I would never do anything to hurt you. Oh, *fuck*!"

He pulls himself off of me and I pull my legs in, curling myself into a ball at the other end in an attempt to get as far away from him as I possibly can. I cannot stop shaking as I sit there half-naked in the middle of a damn parking lot.

What do I do now? Me and my big mouth brought this whole thing upon myself. I watch him through my blurred vision as he straightens himself out and reaches down on the floor. I pray like hell he brings up his knife and kills me, but he doesn't. I am already dead, so he may as well take that knife and plunge it straight through my heart and finish me off.

Instead, he has a rag of some sorts in his hand, and he leans down and wipes himself off with it. He pulls his pants the rest of the way up and then climbs back into the truck, closing the door behind him.

I feel more caged in with him now than I did before as he slides over and presses the rag between my legs as if he is trying to clean me up. What a joke. I will never be clean again. The smell of sex in the air has me gagging and choking beneath the tape.

Maybe he notices, because he drops the rag and removes the tape tenderly. I gasp and suck in as much air as I can. I don't want to look at him and suffer the humiliation any longer, so I turn my head as he finishes wiping me clean and adjusting my clothes back into position.

I risk a look up at him. In my clouded mental state I can't quite figure out the expression spreading across his face. Remorse? Or possibly guilt as he realizes exactly what he has done.

He tries to speak . . . maybe he does say something, I don't know. The last thing I see before I let myself fall into darkness is the look of hatred on his face as he was slamming his body into mine.

Chapter Eighteen

I know I must have completely passed out afterwards, because I come to in the front seat of the truck. My hands are free and I see the sun is hanging much lower toward the horizon.

Looking out of the window, I watch deep gray clouds start to roll in. The sky is as dark as I feel. A deep, black hole where you keep falling and falling with no end in sight, limp and lifeless as a rag doll dragged behind a child and tossed around. The light is right there within reach; I keep clawing and clawing toward it, yet I am retreating further into the darkness as I watch it slip away.

I'm wrecked, a ghost inside my own body. I feel so dirty and I know I have been cast into hell. Trying to sit up, I grimace at the pain shooting through my arms. I manage to pull myself all of the way up and look down at my wrists.

Dark red welts adorn each one. I gently rub them, running my fingers across the rough abrasions. My upper arm has a bruise and feels like it has been pulled out of its socket. My face feels swollen and my head and stomach are throbbing as if I have been hit with a baseball bat. I fight back my tears as I recall in excruciating detail exactly what Trent just did to me.

Never in a million years would I have thought something like this could ever happen to me. How could it? Just a little over a week ago I was living as a happily married woman, working a job I loved and surrounded by a family whose bond I had believed with all my heart was unbreakable. But now it has been broken. No one is going to look at me the same and when they do, it will be with pity.

Turner. How will he ever be able to get past this? He won't. It's bad enough that I slept willingly with Trent, but now he's raped me.

Oh, God! Just the thought of that word has my skin itching. This time I really am going to vomit.

I start coughing and gagging as a wave of nausea grips me.

"Jesus Christ. Are you going to get sick?"

The sound of Trent's voice has me trembling. I turn my head to the window so I don't have to look at him.

"Fucking hell, Clove. You're white as a ghost."

I still say nothing. I can't, and I won't. I have no words for this man who has completely destroyed every part of my world and taken everything I love away from me. I don't even realize we have stopped until my door is pulled open and I feel him put his hands on me. That is when I snap.

"Don't you fucking touch me!"

I recoil farther into the truck. He backs up and holds his hands in surrender, yet I don't trust him.

"There is an outdoor bathroom right here." I follow the direction of his hand and notice we are at a gas station. "Go now."

He turns and walks around to the other side of the truck. Reaching down on the floor I grab my purse and exit the truck as fast as I can. My legs are wobbly as I make the few short steps to the bathroom, keeping my eyes to the ground. I know I look a mess.

Closing the door behind me, I push in the knob to lock it and slump back against the cold steel door. Several minutes pass before I am able to approach the mirror and the sink. I take a few deep breaths before I raise my head and look intently at myself. I am unrecognizable. Both of my cheeks are bruised and swollen. My lip is busted open and my hair is a frizzy mess. I can't control the angry sobs that escape me. Tears stream down my face and sting as they make contact with my lips.

Suddenly having the strong urge to pee, I drop my things onto the floor and enter the stall. When I lift my skirt up and squat to use the bathroom, a small gasp escapes my throat as I see the purple bruises on my upper thighs, but it is nothing compared to the burning sensation racing through the lower half of my body as I try to urinate.

Placing my hands on each side of the stall for support, I finish my business and all of a sudden the nausea is back. I turn around just in time to vomit. Not much comes up because I haven't eaten anything since this morning, but dry heaves wrack my body for a few moments after I've brought up everything I can.

Wiping my mouth with the back of my hand, I take a deep breath, and when I do I can smell him on me. That smell sends me over the edge. I run out of the stall and grab wads and wads of paper towels, then I turn the sink on as hot as I can get it. I pump and pump the liquid soap dispenser, dousing the wet paper towel with it. When I'm done, I push my skirt aside and scrub roughly between my legs, not caring if I am causing further damage to myself.

"Good God," I mutter to myself as I assess the bruising forming on my inner thighs.

There are several of them, and they are tender to the touch. How could someone commit such a terrible act of physical violence? How did I not notice him hurting me like this? This man is going to rot in hell right along with the worst of Satan's spawn of despicable human beings. I hope like hell I am there to witness when that bastard takes his last breath. Better yet, I hope I am the one who sends him to hell because he sure as shit doesn't care if I live the rest of my life there, the crazy motherfucker.

A loud knock on the door makes me freeze with my hand in mid-air. The knocking turns into pounding when I don't answer.

"Clove, if you're not out here in five minutes I will come in there and get you, now hurry the hell up."

He's becoming impatient and not wanting to further delay us from getting wherever the hell it is we are going. Not responding to his command, I take my time getting changed and splash several handfuls of cold water onto my face. There isn't anything more he can do to hurt me at this point. He's crippled me beyond repair with the sadistic things he has done. So yeah, he can fuck off while I try and do my best to clean myself up.

I grab my brush and run it through the knots in my hair until my scalp is sore. After what I know is longer than his five-minute ultimatum, I secure my hair into a ponytail and drop the brush back into my bag. I pull out my toothbrush and toothpaste and scrub the residue of my vomit out of my mouth.

Tossing the items back into my bag, I swing it over my shoulder and grab my purse off of the counter. I take a deep breath as I open the door. I see Trent's form leaning against his truck with his legs crossed at his ankles and his arms crossed over his chest.

I can't even look at him and I sure as shit don't want to sit next to him, either, so I open the door and start to climb in the back. I halt as flashbacks of the rape freeze me to the spot. A chill creeps up my spine and I drop my bags onto the floor in defeat. I raise my eyes after a moment, and that's when I see the long, jagged knife laying on the floorboard of the truck. My eyes go wide and without even thinking, I reach for it and stuff it in my bag.

I can sense him still leaning up against the truck, watching my every move. Dear God up above, please don't let him have seen me pick up that knife. I climb back down and slam the door with as much force as I can and open the front and climb in. After securing my seatbelt, I turn my body completely away from the driver's seat and lay my head up against the window. I close my eyes tight as I feel him enter the truck and start it.

"There's a bag back there with some chips and other munchies I got at the station," Trent says as we accelerate onto the highway.

Fuck him. Even though I am starving, I don't want a damn thing from him. Hearing his voice and being this close in proximity to him has my nerves all over the damn place. So I remain rooted in my spot and ignore him, ticking off every mile marker in my mind. For ten miles, ten damn miles, there is silence and then he reaches over and places his hand on my knee.

The color instantly drains from my face. I try and block out the fact that he has his hand on me and I can't. My breathing becomes ragged. My teeth start chattering and a cold sweat forms on my forehead. I can't seem to get any words to come out of my mouth. I know he must feel me shaking and when his grip tightens on my leg, I tremble more.

"You need to calm down, Clove." His husky voice shoots a bolt of absolute terror through me, starting at the top of my head and traveling through every vein and every organ of my body until it ends at the tips of my toes.

"I'm not going to hurt you. I swear."

Those eight words break through the trance I am under and I take hold of his hand and remove it from me.

"You're not going to hurt me?" I all but whimper as I continue to keep my vision forward.

Out of the corner of my eye, I see him run his hands through his hair as if he is frustrated. Neither of us speaks again for a long time and my mind drifts, until he pulls off onto another exit. My anxiety and panic start all over again as he drives a mile or so down the road through the middle of God knows where before pulling into the parking lot of a rundown, cheap motel.

"W-what are you doing?" I manage to squeak out.

"This is where we are sleeping tonight. Now get out."

He puts the truck in park and exits, taking the keys with him. I don't move and when he turns and notices that I am not behind him, he starts to walk back toward the truck. I promptly open the door as he approaches.

"I have had it up to here with your defiance, Clove. Why do you continue to push me? This would go a hell of a lot smoother for the both of us if you would just do what you're told for once. Jesus, you really must have a death wish."

Yeah, I have a death wish all right, buddy. My wish is for you to fucking die a very slow miserable death.

"Seriously, Trent. If I go in there looking like this, don't you think whoever is working in there is going to suspect something? I mean, look at me. My face looks like I have been beaten up, which I have by the way, and they will suspect *you*. So if you want me to go in there with you, I would say that you're the one with the death wish because not all people go around beating and raping women. Trust me, if you get me around another person I will tell them exactly what you have done to me," I seethe.

"You really don't listen, do you? You must want a repeat performance of what happened a few hours ago."

His face is within an inch of mine now.

"You don't scare me anymore, Trent. You've won. You have broken me and it doesn't matter what you do to me now. I'm as good as dead already."

My hands are clasped together in my lap to hide the fact I am shaking desperately, truly fearing what he may do to me. However, I shrug as if I really don't care. The big problem here is I do care. I want to live to be able to see Turner one last time.

I watch several expressions dance across Trent's face. He knows what I am saying is true. His eyes roam all over my face for several long moments and when they shift lower and land on my wrists, they grow wide as if he is the one who is in shock.

I wish like hell that I knew what he is feeling right now as he brings his gaze back up to meet mine. Is this real remorse for the things he has done? Is he being eaten up by his guilt? I hope he is. I hope it eats away at him until it kills him.

"If you even think about running, I will call my father and have Turner killed immediately, do you understand what I am saying?"

"Where am I going to go? You have us in the middle of nowhere, Trent. And despite what you may think of me, one thing is for certain. I may be an idiot for not letting my brother nab your ass and throw you in jail right where you belong. But what I am is in love with my husband, and I will do anything to see him, as you are already quite aware. And one more thing. There is no need to threaten me again, because I am very well aware of what you are capable of."

He's bewildered by my words, although he says nothing as he spins around and strides into the motel. I scan the parking lot looking for anything or anyone to help me, and it's completely deserted. Only one other car sits in the parking lot and I can only assume it belongs to whoever works here. Slumping back in my seat in defeat, I shake my head back and forth and pray like I have never done before that there are two beds in this room. I don't want to feel his skin touching mine ever again.

Trent returns several minutes later with a key card in his hand along with fresh towels.

"Let's go," he commands as he reaches in the back and pulls out his bag.

I open the car door and slam it shut with a little more force than necessary and retrieve my own bag.

Damn it, the knife is in there. I need to make sure he doesn't see it. Slinging my bag over my shoulder, I follow a small distance behind him until he stops in front of our room and slides the key in. The small light turns green and he pushes the door open. When I enter, I am immediately assaulted with the smell of stale cigarettes and a very strong odor of who the hell knows what.

"Fuck, this place is a dump," Trent mutters as he tosses his bag on the bed.

He walks into the bathroom and closes the door just a fraction. He comes back out within a minute and I hear the shower running.

"Go shower, and make it quick."

Sitting himself down on the bed, he lays back on the pillow, stretching his free arm over the top of his head. He grabs the remote to the television with the other hand, then clicks it on and starts flipping through the channels.

Not saying a word, I grab my bag and make my way into the small bathroom, shutting and locking the door behind me and stripping my clothes off instantly.

Grabbing a towel, I close the lid to the toilet and place the towel on top of it. I check the temp of the water which is a little too hot for my usual shower, but I leave it to try and help burn away all of the remaining traces of what he took from me a few hours earlier. I may be able to erase all of him from my body, but I will never be able to erase what he has done from my mind.

I lean back and let the water soak into my hair, and when it hits my face I brace my hands against the wall as it stings and burns my bruises and cut lip. No longer being able to hold my shit together, I slump down on the floor of the shower, pulling my knees up and placing my chin on top of them. All hell breaks loose as I cry silently in the middle of nowhere. I have never felt so alone in all my life.

Chapter Nineteen

Still trembling, I stumble out of the shower and sway, almost tumbling to my feet. I brace my hand on the wall for support as butterflies course through my veins. After several seconds I steady myself and pick up the towel, drying myself off and slipping my bra and panties on along with a long sleeve t-shirt and a pair of sweatpants.

It didn't dawn on me until just now as I was rifling through my bag that there is only one bed in this room and I know the jerk isn't going to sleep on the stained carpet floor. The thought of sharing a bed with him makes me suddenly become cold and a shudder runs through my body.

I fold up the sundress I had on earlier and stuff it in the bag. The knife catches my attention. I pick it up and raise it sluggishly to my eyes to get a better view. Jagged edges and at least a three-inch blade could do wonders if I had the guts to slice Trent up in his sleep. Bit by bit a smile creeps across my face as I picture him begging for his life while I cut out his black heart.

"If only you had the guts to really do it, Clove," I whisper.

I jump and nearly drop the knife when I hear a banging on the bathroom door.

"Hurry the hell up in there, Clove! Unlock this motherfucking door now!"

What the hell has him so pissed off now? He's so damn angry.

"Clove! Open it now!"

Shoving the blade back into my bag and zipping it up, I unlock the door and swing it open and stare into the eyes of my kidnapper and attacker.

"Don't fucking lock the door again."

He clutches my arms and pulls me flush against his body. He leans in and plants his face into the crook of my neck and sniffs.

"You smell amazing."

I cringe and feel my body go downright frigid as he licks his way up my neck to the base of my ear.

"Don't think for one minute you're fooling me with those baggy fucking excuse for clothes you have on. I know exactly what's underneath them. Besides, no matter what you have on, if I want it then I will damn well take it."

His words make the hair on the back of my neck stand on end. I won't be able to survive another assault. I know I won't. I am already coming apart at the seams piece by piece.

He finally releases me and snatches my bag out of my hands. For the briefest of moments I panic until he takes a step and tosses it onto the floor next to the bed.

"You're going to sit right there while I take my shower," he orders, pointing to the toilet.

"W-why?" I ask.

"Because I don't trust you and because I fucking said so. Now sit!"

He barks orders as if I'm a dog. Maybe I should lift my leg up and piss all over him, too. I mean seriously, where does he think I am going to run off to? I am just about to ask him when he stands directly in front of me and sheds his clothes.

Lowering my head to the floor, I focus on my toes which are still painted a bright shade of pink. Sighing heavily, I remember the first time I came home after spending several hours at the salon getting pampered with a mani/pedi and a massage and waxing everywhere.

Turner's mouth practically fell open as I chucked off my flip-flops and laid on the couch, placing my feet in his lap. He loved this color of pink. He skimmed his hands up my legs until he reached the hem of my jean skirt and slightly lifted it to take a peek underneath. When he saw my smooth pussy, he pounced. Well, smooth and red.

"You did all of this for me?" he asked with such a tender expression on his face. I simply nodded in return.

"God, baby, it must have hurt."

He kept his eyes glued to mine as he gently ran his hands over the top of my mound.

"It hurt like a bitch and I will do it again and again if I get this reaction out of you every time I do it."

I wiggled my toes in his lap as his thick erection stood at full attention. He lifted his eyebrow as if to challenge me.

"Is that so?"

"You know I would anything for you, sweetheart. Anything at all."

And I meant it. I still mean it. I would do anything as long as it gets me back into his arms even for one last time. I will endure all of this pain and suffering. There really are no words to describe the torment I have endured, and after seeing that picture of Turner the other day, I know he is being subjected to some of the same agony I am.

Our love has to be strong enough for us to find our way back to each other and to have our happily ever after. I may have given up all hope of ever being back to the person I was before all of this happened, but I can never give up on true love.

From the very first time I looked into Turner's eyes I knew he was the one for me, and what a wonderful journey it has been. I miss him. The way he touches me, kisses me, and looks at me. I am myself around him and I pray to God that he won't be taken away from me. This horrendous, traumatic web of lies, deceit, and worst of all, betrayal on my part is something I have to live with for the rest of my life, and I will, just as long as I have him standing by my side.

The sound of the shower turning off draws me back to reality. I still don't look up. I simply can't. I can feel his eyes bore into me as he takes hold of his towel. There isn't a sound to be heard except for him rustling around drying himself off.

"You need to eat something, Clove."

His demanding tone makes my blood start to boil. Yes, I am starving and extremely thirsty, but if I yield to him and eat, I know I won't be able to hold it down. I shrug and keep my eyes glued to the floor.

"You're making this situation harder on yourself than it needs to be," he says as he walks past me and out into the small, musty motel room.

Now that he is finished with his shower, does this mean I can get up or am I supposed to stay here until he orders me to move? I hear him shuffling around in his black duffel bag he brought in with him and decide I am going to sit here until either he comes in and gets me or I know for sure he is dressed. Seeing him without any clothes on is a mental picture I can live without.

I nearly jump out of my skin when I hear a knock on the door. I go to stand up when he hollers for me to stay put. I stay standing in the middle of the bathroom floor listening to him say thank you and keep the change. He must have ordered some food. I get my answer as I take a large whiff and the aroma of pizza fills my nostrils. My stomach knows there is food and lets out a large growl.

Shutting off the light in the tiny bathroom, I round the small dividing wall and almost stumble right into Trent, who is standing there with his nostrils flaring and his fists clenched tightly to his sides. Taking a step back and out of his reach, I start trembling so badly I don't think I will ever stop. I shake my head back and forth as if to say no, but he presses forward. I move backwards until I am resting up against the wall.

"You're really starting to piss me off with this bullshit game you seem to be playing by not talking or eating. Now I am only going to say this one more time, and unless you want a repeat performance of earlier today, you will go sit your ass on that bed and eat."

He points his finger in the direction of the bed and my eyes follow.

"You're right."

I stand tall and defiant. I do need to eat. I definitely don't want him to put his hands on me ever again, and I need the strength to fight. Stepping aside so I can make my way past him, I plop my ass on the bed and cross my legs. I lift up the lid of the pizza box, and oh God, the smell of it makes me realize I am famished.

Not giving a shit, I pick up a piece and devour it like the starving woman I am. Opening one of the bottles of water that is lying next to the box of pizza, I down it and grab one more slice. I scooch my body back until I hit the headboard and then stretch my legs out in front of me. Like a good little girl obeying her parents, I finish off my pizza as I watch Trent grab the box and sit at the small table next to the window.

Within five minutes he has the rest of the pizza gone and tosses the box onto the floor. He slumps back in his chair. His body language gives away the fact that he is frustrated as he runs his hands down his face and then rubs the back of his neck. Welcome to the club, asshole.

Minutes tick by in this small, confined room and I start to shake my foot for no particular reason at all.

"We need to talk about a few things I need from you, Clove."

He breaks the spell of silence. What could he possibly need from me? This is the second time he has mentioned this. What could I possibly have to do with him getting his hands on all those stupid fucking millions of dollars he craves?

"I don't know what I have that you need or how I can help you in any way."

Truthfully I couldn't care less what he thinks he needs from me, but then again, this isn't about me. I need to get my head out of my ass and get it on straight to try and get to Turner, so I plaster on what has got to be the fakest smile in all of fake smile history as I turn and look at him.

"What is it you need?"

Good girl, Clove. You sounded strong and confident, and even though you are dying inside, do not look away from him.

He already knows you're scared to death of him and he could crush you completely again and leave you with absolutely nothing. With a will I didn't even know I possessed, I hold his stare with icy, hate-filled eyes.

"I need my brother's signature on a few documents and he refuses. You are the only one who I believe can make him sign."

His smug look and attitude have me laughing inside. I'll be damned. Trent and his dear old dad can't do a damn thing without Turner's signature. If my husband has refused, then I need to play the rest of this game out right. There is no way in fucking hell I will make him sign a damn thing.

Until I see my husband, I am going to make a few demands of my own. This bastard is going to do exactly what I say. I muster my courage and swing my legs off of the side of the bed. When I turn and meet his gaze again, I enjoy seeing the wind taken out of his sails. I stick my hand out.

"If you want me to help you, then let me talk to my husband."

"You've got to be fucking kidding me if you think I am handing over my phone to you and letting you talk to my brother. Are you entirely clueless as to how serious this is, Clove? Well, let me fill you in on just how severe and life threatening this whole situation is. Come sit."

He twists in his chair and pats the bed directly in front of him.

"I am not a damn dog so I would appreciate it if you would quit treating me like one and ordering me to sit. This room is like a jail cell, Trent. I can hear you just fine from right here."

His head slowly goes down and he looks utterly defeated. I just stand there, lost. When he brings his gaze back up to mine, his eyes are full of unshed tears.

"Clove, I- I am sorry for what I did to you. I have no explanation for it. I did it, and I have to live with it. I am not going to ask you to forgive me because I know you won't. I mean, how could you, right?" he scoffs. "Please sit down and let me explain things to you. Please."

For the first time he is pleading with me. My legs move toward the bed and I sit at the edge as far away from him as possible. I have no choice but to listen to him, but no matter what he has to say to me, I will never forgive him for the brutal attack he forced me to endure.

So, he wants me to understand the reasons behind why he is doing all of this? I know I will never be able to understand, and I don't really want to. He has taken a part of my soul and I will never get it back.

I keep trying to convince myself this was not my fault, but a part of me says it is. I will always think, 'what if I did this?' or 'what if I did that?' I will never be able to trust my own judgment again. My self-respect is destroyed beyond repair. I will never be my father's little girl anymore or my brother's little sister. I will always be Clove, the victim. Clove, the woman who slept with her husband's brother. Clove, the woman who "allowed" herself to get raped.

I hate myself. Truly hate myself. The only thing I have to live for right now is making sure I do everything I possibly can to help Turner get out of this alive. So with this war currently waging inside my body, I steel myself and face the man who has won the battle.

"I'm listening. Explain."

Chapter Twenty

"You've shocked me, Clove."

"And why is that?"

He props one of his arms on the table, his gaze drifting from me to the door and then back again.

"For as long as I can remember, my father has tainted my life against both my mother and my brother. I have always believed my mother didn't want me. Dad used to always tell me she favored my brother over me and they would fight over it all the time until one day he got sick and tired of her smacking me around and packed up our bags and left."

Brainwashed with a bunch of lies. I'm not surprised, considering what I know about his father. James would have done everything possible to ensure Trent's unconditional loyalty. I don't say anything, though. I just let him continue on with his story.

"I have tried and tried to remember my life when the four of us lived together. The very few memories I have are of my brother always being clumsy and me picking him up so we could continue doing whatever it was we were doing. I have tried more times than I can count to bring even the smallest details into my mind, and nothing. That's it. I didn't even remember what my mother looked like until a few years ago when Dad and I finally decided it was time to start putting this plan into motion."

He's like a small child sitting over there in the overstuffed chair as he mourns his lack of memories with grief written all over him. If I didn't hate him as much as I do, I would actually feel sorry for him. All he knows is what he was told by his cruel father, and it is far from the truth, I know it is. Melody loved both of her sons more than life itself. She grieved every day for Trent. I continue to sit there in silence; saying nothing at this point is for the best.

"My dad was a good dad, except for when he would go on one of his drinking binges. Then all hell would break loose. Sometimes his spells would last for weeks at a time. He would bring countless whores over to our house and I would hear them in his room all times of the day and night. Shit . . . for my sixteenth birthday present, my dad arranged for one of his many sluts to wait for me in bed, naked and spread wide open. A teenage boy staring down at a piece of ass just waiting to be fucked? I was all over that shit. I thought I was living the good life, with pussy anytime I wanted waiting for me almost every day when I walked in from school."

He shakes his head then rests it on the back of his chair, staring up at the ceiling.

"Did he work?" I blurt out.

"Who, my dad?" He starts to laugh. "If you want to call dealing and selling drugs work, then yes, he worked. My dad is one scary son of a bitch, Clove. Even now in his old age, he scares the shit out of me."

"Was he abusive to you too? I mean, when you were growing up?"

"Fuck, up until I could actually fight back, that prick slapped me around any time he fucking felt like it. One day I punched him hard enough that he actually fell on his drunken, drug-riddled ass."

He chuckles grimly at the memory before going on.

"I was raised by a drunk and a drug addict, that's all I have ever known. When I was old enough to start dealing and making my own money, I did. At the age of eighteen I thought I had it all, living the good life. The dough kept rolling in, right along with any and every kind of piece of ass I wanted. You wouldn't believe the kinds of shit chicks would do just to get their next fix."

My eyes go wide and I freeze. I feel like the walls of the room are closing in on me. Shit! I have had unprotected sex with this man! He has been with God knows how many women and they have been with God knows how many men.

The realization makes me want to vomit. Trent senses something is wrong; he inches closer to me and kneels on the floor alongside the bed.

"Clove, what is it? You're as white as a ghost."

My hand comes up and covers my mouth. *Oh, God!*

"You fucker!" I scream as I remove my hand and shove him backwards.

"Clove, what the fuck?" he growls, pulling himself up to his full height and towering over me.

"H-how many women have you slept with?" I shriek, my voice breaking in panic.

Understanding dawns on Trent's face.

"Clove, I swear to you! I have always used a condom with everyone except you. I may be a lot of things, but ignorant is not one of them. I am clean. If anything, you have to believe that."

His eyes silently plead his case, asking for mercy. I have none to give as I gaze back at him with hatred. Finally, he looks away.

"I know my word means nothing to you, Clove. Believe me when I say I don't blame you at all. You don't think I see how much you hate me when you look at me? Don't you see? That's the hardest part of this whole, fucked up mess," he says, looking down at his side dejectedly.

What does he mean by that?

"Hate isn't even a strong enough word for what I feel for you. I don't think one even exists, Trent, but if there was I would multiply it a million times over, that I can assure you."

"Like I said, I don't blame you at all. I hate myself for what I have done to you, Clove. I have been obsessed with you since the first time I laid eyes on you a few years ago."

I am so taken back by what he just said that I jump off the bed in shock.

"Jesus Christ! You mean to tell me you have been following us for over two years? What the fuck is wrong with you?" I scream loudly.

"Keep your damn voice down! You said you were going to listen to me, so sit back down and listen, because I am far from fucking done!"

He then sits in silence for a moment, as if he is choosing his next words carefully.

"For the first few months, all I did was follow you around. I was so caught up in your beauty and innocence. I had never seen a woman carry herself with such grace and confidence in my whole life. Every time I saw you tuck a strand of your hair behind your ear, I wanted it to be my hands doing it for you. Seeing the way your face would light up whenever you would look at my brother would have me lying in bed at night pretending it was me instead of him. And fuck me for being the perverted prick that I am, but every time I would hear you moaning out your pleasure as I stood at the foot of your stairs listening to you making love with my brother, my hands would inch towards my gun, because I wanted so badly to climb those stairs and kill him as I screamed out that you were mine. Not his, not anyone else's. Just mine."

My head slowly starts to shake back and forth as I realize he is speaking the God's honest truth for the first time since I have met him. He thinks he loves me? He has no clue what love really means. One minute he is raping me and beating the shit out of me, and the next he is telling me he wants me to be his alone. What the hell? This twisted motherfucker sitting before me has lost his damn mind.

Choosing my next words carefully is not easy. I cannot even begin to fully process what he has just confessed to me.

The man has stalked me, broken into my home, and listened to my husband and me in our most intimate moments. He has invaded my life in a warped and disturbing way, and yet he sits there and feels comfortable coming clean about his feelings for me. What the hell kind of game is he playing at?

"Say something, Clove. Anything. Just say something."

I stare blankly at him. After what he has just thrown at me, I am supposed to say something?

"I don't know what you want me to say, Trent. Do you understand the absurdity of what you are saying to me? Do you actually hear yourself right now? When one person cares for another, they don't do the vile and heartless things to that person that you have done, Trent. They don't beat them and they sure as hell don't rape them! Look at me! Look at what you have done! You have destroyed me. I'm broken beyond repair."

Trent rakes his hands through his hair in frustration.

"I told you, that wasn't me back there in my truck earlier! And as far as smacking you around and the brutal things I said to you at your house, I panicked. I had to do what I had to do to make you listen to me. Look, Clove, I don't think you get what I am saying here. I am saying that you and I could have the world at our feet with this money. If you would just listen to my plan, we could escape from here and no one would ever find us."

I just gape at him with my mouth hanging open at the sheer audacity of this piece of shit. Does he actually think I would leave my husband and run away with him? I could never love a man like him, let alone run away with him and live my life on the lam. What kind of life would that be? There is no amount of money in this entire fucked up world that we live in that could ever make me want to do that.

The silence hanging in the air between us becomes uncomfortable as Trent waits for me to speak. As I continue to say nothing, he begins to plead with me.

"Listen, please. I have a plan. If you help me and it works out, this plan could save Turner's life. After all of these years of my father drilling into me over and over again how much my mother hated me, I know it's not true. It's not. He doesn't deserve a dime of this money, not one red cent. He deprived me of a normal, loving childhood with my mother and my brother, and my plan is to kill him."

Wait, what? Kill James? I don't know if Trent is trying to mind-fuck me or if he actually believes what he is saying. All I do know is that the only way I am going to have any shot at all of getting Turner and myself away from this madness is by pretending to go along with whatever maniacal plan Trent has concocted.

I don't feel at all remorseful at the fact that Trent is planning to kill his father. He is the one who has orchestrated all of this and as far as I am concerned, he can burn in the hottest fires of hell for what he has done. He sounds even more screwed up than Trent is. If he loathes Turner, who is his own child, I can only imagine what he thinks of me. What might he try to do when we come face to face?

I need to clear my thoughts and the only way to do this right now is to try and get some rest. With that in mind, I take a deep breath and talk to my nemesis in a calm and controlled voice.

"You cannot expect me to just give you an answer right now, Trent. This is more than I can handle right now. It's too much to process and I need to think. I need more information than, 'oh, I have a plan and we are going disappear with millions of dollars in our pockets.' It doesn't work like that. Have you thought about where we would go, and what we would do with all of that money? This isn't the movies; you can't just hop on a plane with millions of dollars in a suitcase and head for the nearest island."

I shake my head in exasperation.

"And what about my family? Do you have any idea what this has to be doing to them right now? You say you were deprived of a loving home, and I cannot even begin to fathom what that must be like, but I wasn't. You say you have watched me for years? So then you know how much my family means to me and how much I mean to them."

He looks up at me with suspicion, but I see a gleam of hope deep in his eyes.

"What exactly are you saying, Clove?"

What I'm saying is that you have your head so far up your damn ass that you will most likely get all of us killed with this preposterous game you're playing, I think to myself. What I say out loud is,

"You have given me a lot to think about. I just feel like I need to know more of what you are thinking. I mean, stop and think about everything you just told me, Trent. Are you planning to go waltzing into wherever it is we are going and just point a gun at your dad and kill him? He doesn't seem the type of person to be taken out so easily. And how do you really think you are going to get your hands on the money? I mean come on, you and Turner's fingerprints don't even match, for God's sake. How in the hell do you think my brother found out who you were?"

"So you know I have a rap sheet. So what?" He shrugs. "It's all petty crimes, mostly stealing food when I fucking needed it because my dad would be too damn drunk or too fucked up on drugs to notice there wasn't any around. The only time we ever had food in our house would be when one of his whores would come over and feel sorry for the scrawny ass kid who was starving half to death. Back then I didn't have a damn choice but to try and take care of myself, but now I do. Somehow, some way, I am going to get that money. My only wish is that once I have it, you will come along with me for the ride of a lifetime, Clove."

I stand there fighting the urge to actually commit a crime for the first time in my life and choke the hell out of him.

"Oh for fuck's sake, Trent," I say, glaring daggers at him. "I can't deal with this half-assed plan of yours anymore. I need to get some sleep and we will talk about this in the morning."

"You're right; I haven't fully planned this out. The only thing I do know for sure is that I am not giving you up. No fucking way, not when I finally have you. I have never had any kind of beauty in my entire fucked up life, and I knew once I had a taste of you, I would not be able to let you go."

He stands and points his finger at me.

"So. Either we figure this out together and you come away with me, or, after I get my hands on that money, and trust me I will get my hands on it, I will kill my brother. The choice is yours. Now, since you're so adamant and I can't trust you . . ."

He bends down and scoops his bag up off the floor, striding in my direction. I watch in horrid fascination as he pulls out a pair of handcuffs and securely snaps one of the manacles shut around my wrist.

"What are you doing?" I half shriek as he secures the other one to his own wrist.

"I may have confessed a lot of shit to you, Clove, and I am just as ready as you are for a good night's sleep, but I'm not a fool."

He lifts our now joined hands.

"This is my way of making sure you don't decide to skip out on me while we sleep."

Chapter Twenty-One

Lying flat on my back shackled to a loudly snoring Trent was not my idea of rest, I must say. I may as well try and come up with some sort of plan. The only thing I can think of is to somehow contact my brother and hope he can find us in time. That's it; there is nothing else I can do. But how? How am I going to be able to get away from this psycho when he watches my every move?

If I am not able to reach my family, will James kill us both if or when he realizes his plan isn't going to work? Of course he will; to think he won't is foolish. Once he figures out that neither Turner nor I will help them, he will have no further use for either one of us. And if James figures out that Trent is planning on double-crossing him, God only knows what will happen.

Speaking of Trent, what about his 'obsession' with me, as he calls it? If I don't go along with him willingly he will kill Turner out of pure spite, I have no doubt about it. This shit is more fucked up than I could ever have imagined.

If Trent hates his father as much as he said he does, why didn't he just show up at our doorstep, or even Melody's, and tell us who he was? God, all of this could have been avoided and he could have had his money and a family who would have loved him more than anything. So the question of the fucking day is, why the hell is he *really* doing this? These thoughts circle around and around in my mind until I finally feel myself drift off to sleep.

****

The sun is already up and shining; my eyes open to the bright light pouring through the crack of the drapes. I go to stretch and try to lift my arms when the clink of a metal chain reminds me that I am still cuffed to Trent.

I nudge him hard to wake him up.

"Good morning," he says huskily.

Fuck him and his good morning. It's anything *but* a good morning. It's another day in hell for me.

"I have to pee. Can you uncuff me, please?"

He says nothing, but reaches into his jeans pocket and pulls out the key. My wrist feels tight and numb when he drops it to my lap after unlocking the cuffs. My free hand automatically goes to rub it and to try to bring back the blood flow.

Hoisting myself out of bed, I gather my bag up off the floor and make my way into the bathroom. When I go to lock the door, I hesitate as I remember him telling me to keep it unlocked.

I spend as little time in the bathroom as possible, brushing my hair and pulling it into a ponytail, then getting dressed in my last pair of clean shorts and an oversized t-shirt. I stuff the knife back in my bag underneath my dirty clothes. I brush my teeth and stow everything back into the bag.

When I step out into the room, Trent is on the phone talking quietly. I toss my bag onto the bed and sit on the edge. My ears perk up as I hear him say we will be there later this afternoon. Where is 'there,' I wonder? Is it where Turner is?

The possibility of being able to see him today brightens my gloomy mood even though I have no idea what kind of state he is going to be in when I get there. The only thing that matters to me at this moment is being able to finally see him with my own eyes.

When I hear Trent finally ending his call, I stand and direct my attention to him. He slips a worn out gray t-shirt over his head and then bends down to retrieve his shoes.

"I just need to use the bathroom and brush my teeth and then we are out of here," he states, and rummages through his bag for his toothbrush and paste.

He marches past me avoiding any contact, and I sense his mood has dampened as he strides with purpose into the bathroom, leaving the door open.

Taking a seat at the small, round table he just vacated, my bottom feels something hard as I sit. When I reach underneath me to see what it is. It's his phone! My hands shake as I stare blankly at the screen. I slide my finger across the screen and try to open it. Shit, shit, shit! He has it locked.

My mind scrambles to try and think of what his password could be. I start frantically pressing in random four digits in hopes I can come up with the right one. Nothing works. I have no clue. And that is when I see the pad of paper and a pen on the table. Wasting no time at all, I scribble as fast as I can my brother's phone number, my name, and that I have been kidnapped and to please call this number. As I hear the water shut off, I place the phone back on the chair and turn the notepad upside down. I quickly sit myself back on the edge of the bed.

Trent strolls out and throws his items back in his bag, grabbing his phone in the process. Beads of sweat form on the back of my neck as I watch him closely as he zips up his bag and looks around the table as if he is making sure he has everything. He notices his phone in the chair and picks it up, studying it for several drawn out seconds.

My heart rate picks up speed as he turns to look at me. I look right back at him with what I hope is my best 'I didn't do anything' look. A sigh of relief escapes me as he grabs both of our bags and instructs me to get up. I do as I am told and he holds the door open for me as we walk out into the bright sun. Instantly my vision blurs. I wish I could feel as bright and cheery as this beautiful day is. Instead, I feel dark and depressed, just like an overcast sky heralding a storm that will destroy everything in its path.

Trent unlocks the doors and tosses everything in the back as we climb into this truck. The truck I wish I could burn right along with the man who owns it. We drive for almost an hour before he finally speaks.

"I need gas again." He pulls off another exit and into the parking lot of a gas station. "Stay put and I'll get some coffee and something to eat."

Jesus, what the hell is his problem all of a sudden? He slams the truck door and rounds the back to start pumping his gas. That phone call with his dad must have put him in a shit mood. Something has happened and it's obvious it is something he doesn't like.

Please God, don't let it be anything to do with Turner. But something tells me it's not. Maybe there has been a change of plans and he doesn't agree with them. I have no clue, but one thing is for certain. I am going to ask him.

When he comes back, he hands me a large, steaming cup of coffee. I have never wanted coffee so much in my entire life. He hands me a bag with a couple of breakfast sandwiches as he starts to take off back toward the highway. Ten miles or so down the road we enter   Mississippi.
Taking a small sip of my coffee and the last bite of my sandwich, I contemplate how to approach his mood.

"I overheard you on the phone briefly before we left. I assume it was your dad you were talking to. Did something happen?"

My voice cracks and my hands grip the coffee cup tightly.

"Something like that," he says, leaving me to wallow in my curiosity.

"Um. Care to share?"

"You're not going to like it any more than I do, but there isn't a damn thing I can do about it until we get to where we need to go."

I twist my body in the seat to face him.

"And where is it we're going?"

He gives me a 'shut up and I will tell you' look.

"Zack has put out an APB on you. You're all over the news, along with me, my father, and this whole fucking story."

He slams his fist up against the steering wheel and presses down on the gas pedal. I keep my face impassive, but inside I am laughing like a lunatic. What the hell did they expect? For my family to just lie down and say, 'oh, go ahead, you can just take Clove and we will be okay with never seeing or hearing from her again'?

Angling my entire body toward the window, my thoughts turn positive. I have no idea what kind of connections my brother has with cops outside his jurisdiction, but my guess would be once he receives the phone call from the hotel, if he hasn't already, he will be on the road like Trent's worst nightmare, and the asshole knows it as he continues his rant.

"Fucking Zack! He's fucked this whole thing up, and my dad is pissed off at both me and you and . . . FUCK!" he screams into the truck, making me jump and press myself further back into my seat.

For miles and miles after his outburst, he doesn't say another word. Every once in a while I risk a glance at him out of the corner of my eye. His forehead is scrunched and the muscles in his jaw are clenched so damn tight that I can practically see the wheels in head turning. I cave and break the silence.

"So are we heading to where your father is, or what?"

"Fuck, yes. We're going to where they are. You don't know my dad, Clove. If I don't show up there with you, he will not hesitate to put a damn bullet through your husband's head. And trust me sweetheart, it won't be pretty," he declares.

"Good God, Trent. I just don't understand how the two of you could be so hateful toward your own flesh and blood."

I knew the minute I opened my mouth I should have kept quiet. His glare swings towards me and his hand flies out, grasping me by my ponytail and yanking me in his direction.

"You will never understand shit! It's not about the money anymore. You're so concerned about my brother that you don't see I am trying to save his fucking life here! For the love of Christ, woman, shut your damn mouth so I can think of a way to get your fucking husband out of that damn house."

He shoves me back and even though my head is hurting like a bitch from his death grip on my hair, I can see a sliver of light through this cloud of darkness. This isn't another one of his ploys to get me on his side. Trent means exactly what he says.

Not another word passes between us until we pull into a small town just outside Jackson, Mississippi. I have tried my best to keep track of where we are going in case Turner and I get the chance to escape. I've watched every turn, taken notice of every landmark or point of interest.

We pull off onto a dirt drive and continue to follow it until we are invisible from the road. Trent comes to a sudden stop. Putting the truck into park, he keeps his eyes locked straight ahead and his hands on the steering wheel, gripping tighter and tighter as the seconds tick by.

My senses perk up as I feel something pulling me forward. I can feel Turner close by, almost as if I can hear him calling to me. It's a strange sensation, feeling him near me. It's love. In spite of my fear and anxiety, I feel excitement. I want to jump out of this truck and run to him and tell him I am here and I am alive.

What the hell is Trent doing just sitting here? We need, no, *I* need to get to Turner. He needs me, I can feel it. I can't stay caged in this truck any longer knowing my husband is close by.

"Trent?" I whisper.

"What, Clove?" He cranks his body in my direction and with icy eyes stares me down.

"What are we doing here?" I ask, trying to play dumb to get him to move his ass, no matter what is waiting down the end of this fucking road.

"They're down there, aren't they?"

"Yes, they are," he says simply, his tone of voice for the first time truly indicating fear.

"Trent, I have no idea what the hell we are about to walk into. You need to clue me in on what is going on here and what you want me to do, or I swear, I'll-"

"You'll what, Clove? Go marching in there and demand that my father hand over Turner and let you walk out of there alive? You're out of your fucking mind if you think that will ever happen. I know him, and I will guarantee you he is drunk as a motherfucker in there. He is not a man to mess with when he is fucked up like that. Damn it all to hell, I have no clue if Turner is even still alive!"

All of the blood drains from my face and I lose all train of thought except for what just came out of Trent's mouth, but then my intuition kicks back in.

"He's not dead!" I blurt.

"No. Something tells me he's not either. I am sorry I even said it, but you have to understand what we are about to walk into here."

I shiver, trying not to let his words frighten the life out of me.

"You need to stay as close to me as possible when we go in there." He reaches across the console and grips my hand, giving it a light squeeze. "Come on, Clove. Come back to me and listen. Where is that smart mouthed girl from just a few hours ago?"

Trent places his hand under my trembling chin and raises it so my gaze meets his. God, I don't want his hands on me anywhere after everything that he has done, and yet I know instinctively he is the only one who can get both Turner and me out of here alive.

I hate having to rely on him for anything at all. I know he knows this as he watches my changing expressions. He looks away for a few moments as if he is trying to collect his own thoughts and releases both my chin and my hand.

Even though the sky is turning gray with clouds, and even though the deep shadows of the woods surround us, I can still see his eyes glimmering with tears. I don't feel sorry for him. He deserves every bit of pain he is in, and more.

Chapter Twenty-Two

"You really hate me that much, don't you?" His words cut through the silence in the truck.

"Do we really have to sit here and talk about this, Trent?"

"No, I guess not. I deserve your hatred, Clove. This I know. A man can only hope, though. Right?"

He shrugs and starts up the truck. We are driving toward God knows what and a part of me screams with joy that I will see Turner soon. However, a bigger part of me is intimidated as all hell at the mere thought of what could happen to me before I get the chance.

After a short but very bumpy ride, we find ourselves parked outside of what has to be the most run-down house I have ever seen. The porch light is lit, chasing away the gloom and making every miserable inch of this place visible.

I gape at the front porch and the stairs that are missing several boards, which would cause an unwary person to fall right through. The white paint on the siding is chipped and peeling, several windows are broken, and the roof is covered in a thick layer of moss that appears to be growing up the side of the house.

I feel like I am staring at some haunted mansion. I am sure that once upon a time it was a beautiful little home, but this place is so bad now as to be unlivable. From what I can see of the yard, the grass has grown up so high it reaches over the top of the windowsills.

Oh, God. Did Trent grow up here like this? I envision a small boy running around here playing outside. Did he ever have anyone to play with? My heart breaks for the little boy who never deserved to have a life like this. And Turner. He's been here for how long, now? Is there even running water in this place? Food? Obviously the electricity works, but good Lord almighty, how could anyone live this way? Tears spring to my eyes as I take it all in.

"The outside looks a lot worse than it does on the inside, Clove."

I jerk my head around and face a somber looking Trent.

"Did you grow up here?" I sniff as I wipe away the tears from my face with the back of my hand.

"No. I grew up in Jackson, actually. This place used to be halfway decent when I was younger. Dad and I used to come out here and hunt all the time. Some of the very few times my dad was sober would be when he hunted. For whatever fucked up reason, that man was serious about his hunting. Especially deer and pheasant. I fucking hated it. But it was the only time I ever got to spend time with my real dad, you know?" He looks at the house as if lost in his memories before finally turning back toward me. His face turns serious as he opens his truck door. "You ready?"

I nod, still a little shaken.

"Stay close to me, Clove. And whatever you do, for the love of Christ, keep your mouth shut and only talk to him when he talks to you."

Glaring at me, he steps out of the truck and shuts his door. I can't move and I swallow the biggest lump in my throat as I try and force my unstable hands to reach for the door handle. Immediately Trent is right there opening the door for me, and places his hands on my shoulders as if he is trying to comfort me. Even though I hate having him touch me, at this moment in time he is the only comfort I have. He looks deeply into my eyes; searching for what, I have no idea.

"One more thing. I promise I will do anything I can to keep you safe, but if something happens to me, here is a spare key to the truck. You have got to promise me you will get the hell out of here and run, whether you have Turner with you or not. Promise me, Clove," he commands, shaking my shoulders for emphasis.

"I- I don't know if I can do that," I say, my voice barely a whisper. He starts to shake my shoulders a little more vigorously.

"You have to promise me, Clove! I will get back in this truck and tie you down and we will leave, and I mean it if you DO. NOT. PROMISE. ME."

Jesus God Almighty, what the hell are we walking into?

"I promise," I say sullenly. One thing I know for certain; I will fight until my last breath before I walk out of here without my husband.

"Good girl."

He releases his grip on my shoulders and grabs my hand as he helps me down. I grip tightly to his as he carefully leads me up the short, narrow path and the creaky stairs. As soon as we land on the top step, the door swings wide open and for the first time I come face to face with the man who created my husband.

"Well, well, well. If it isn't my long lost son and the fucking princess herself," he slurs slightly, wobbling.

James looks nothing like the man in the pictures I saw from years ago. His teeth are rotting, his face is pale, and oh God, his eyes. Even though they are bloodshot and halfway closed, they are the most terrifying pair of eyes I have ever seen. Eyes that say, 'I know exactly what scares you, bitch, and it's me.' They bore into me with hostility and contempt. As skinny as he is you would think he would be easy to snap in half, but those eyes make you think twice about ever trying to fuck with him.

"I thought I told you to kill that fucking bitch, boy?" He straightens his posture as he glowers from me to Trent. "Does she have you fucking pussy whipped just like your fucking pussy ass brother? If so, maybe dear old dad should have a taste, too? Spread it around between the three of us before I fucking slice her into a million pieces."

He rakes his eyes slowly up and down my body, allowing his gaze to linger on my chest. I cower closer to Trent and try and hide myself behind him as best as I can. I have never been so petrified in my life. And he can sense it as he stands there and laughs evilly.

"Bitch, he ain't gonna save you from me."

He lifts a bottle that I never saw in his hands to his dirty mouth and takes a heavy swig. I feel Trent's body tense as I stand behind him. Is he just going to stand here and not say a damn word? I want in this house and I want to see Turner more than I have ever wanted anything in my entire life. I nudge him in his back slightly, trying to give him a hint. Finally he speaks.

"Dad, I told you on the phone I wasn't going to do a damn thing to her no matter what you said to me, and I meant it. She gets out of here without a hair on her head touched or we will never be able to get out of this fucked up mess alive."

"Who the fuck do you think you are, you little bastard? You don't call the shots here, I do. I brought you into this world, you fucking punk ass bitch, and I sure as fuck won't hesitate to take you the fuck out of it."

He spits all over the damn place when he spews his fowl words at his son. Even though I am scared shitless, I am about ready to tell this asshole where he can shove it. It's no wonder this man I am clinging onto as if my life depends on it is the way he is. James Calloway is a repulsive human being. He evokes the deepest form of hatred in my being.

"You're drunk, Dad. When was the last time you had something to eat?" Trent asks kindly.

I don't know if he is being sincere or not. I am sure a part of him cares about this man standing in front of us, but who gives a flying fuck if he eats or not? I sure as hell don't.

"What do you care boy? You gonna make me some food?"

James laughs as he turns around and staggers into the house. Trent grabs my hand and pulls me forward with him. When the smell of the inside of this house assaults my senses, I have to place my free hand over my nose. The acrid smell burns my nostrils and I can taste it deep in my throat. It smells old, dusty, and damp. Rancid, even. The door slams shut with a loud squeak and I jump. Trent squeezes my hand as if trying to reassure me.

We walk deeper into the room. There is a small kitchen table with a few mismatched chairs and a kitchen off to the right. Dirty dishes cover every surface in sight. No wonder it smells in here, it's just as filthy on the inside as it is on the outside. The white fridge is covered in a thick layer of black dust.

There are piles of shit everywhere, from papers to empty pizza boxes, all strewn across the table. Beer bottles and cans and empty liquor bottles in clear plastic bags are piled up in one corner while in another corner sits a small round table with a bag of white powder, razor blades, and rolled up dollars. Holy shit, it's cocaine! This is the shit pile my husband has been kept in. I feel my blood start to boil looking at this damn mess. This place needs to be burned to the damn ground with this smug ass bastard in it.

"So what do you propose we do now, boy? Now that this bitch has fucked it all up for us and that money is good as flushed down the fucking toilet?"

"Come on, Dad. You know it's not her fault. Jesus, can't you stay off of the damn booze for one damn day so we can figure out how to get the hell out of here before the cops show up?"

Trent speaks as if he is pleading for this piece of shit's help.

"You hearing me, Trent? WHAT THE FUCK DO WE DO NOW? I say we kill that bastard son of mine in the other room, and then kill his pretty little wife. After I fuck her, first."

As soon as I hear him say Turner is in the other room, I lose all sense of reason. I loosen my grip on Trent and move in front of him.

"Where the hell is my husband?" I scream and start to storm towards the only hallway in the house.

"Clove! Get back here!" Trent bellows from behind me. I run the few short steps it takes to get to the only closed door, but before I can reach for the doorknob I am suddenly jerked from behind and lifted up off of the ground.

"Trent! Put me down, now! He's in there. God, let me go! Please!" I cry as I kick and scream and try to claw at his arms. He's too strong, though. He carries me back into the small living room and sets me down on the ratty, filthy couch.

"Sit down and shut your damn mouth."

Trent points his finger at me. I hear unintelligible words spouting forth from the chair where his father is sitting.

"You are one crazy ass fucking bitch if you think I am letting you anywhere near him. Not until I am finished with you first." James stands and staggers backwards bracing his hands on the arms of the chair.

"Fuck you! You're the crazy one here, not me!"

I have had it with his insults. Fuck him! He wants to continue to call me a bitch? I will show him what this bitch can do.

"Fuck you, you fucking slobbering spineless dick! The money doesn't even belong to you. It never has and it never will. You're nothing but a little weasel who has hidden behind his drugs and booze all of his life. Who the hell do you think you are? You've all but destroyed both of your sons' lives. What kind of person separates their child from their mother and their brother? Brings them up like you did Trent, showing them not one ounce of love whatsoever. You're a real piece of work with your evil, corrupted, warped mind!"

A thunderous rage seeps out of James' eyes, and his fists clench at his sides as I finish my little speech. When he speaks, I begin to realize I should have just done exactly what Trent told me to.

"This is my house, and women speak when they are told to speak, and not before. And they sure as fuck don't call me crazy. But since you think I am crazy, let me show you just how crazy I can be."

Before I can even blink, James strikes me right in the jaw with his fist. My head snaps back from the blow, slamming me into the wall. For the longest time I can't move as pain radiates from my cheek and mouth and the taste of blood dissolves on my tongue.

"Get her the hell out of my face until I decide what the hell I am going to do with her."

I open my eyes and his gaze is murderous and unblinking as a deadly viper. Trent quickly scoops me up into his arms and carries me down the short hallway. He stops at the open doorway directly across from the room I know Turner is in. I try to hear any kind of noise coming from that room and there is nothing. Could he be dead, or close to it? I panic and forget about my throbbing face. Trent carries me through the doorway and lays me calmly on top of a bed.

"Do you want to get yourself killed, Clove? Because you are heading in that very direction. I told you to keep quiet, and I meant it. You're damn lucky he hasn't killed you yet! He knows there is no reason to keep you alive so now, you're stuck in this damn room until I can figure out what the hell to do."

He turns to leave and I stamp down my anger for a brief minute or two.

"Trent, you have to go in there and make sure Turner is alive. Please?" I start crying and sobbing uncontrollably.

"Get your fucking ass out here now and leave that bitch!" James shouts.

"Fucking Christ. Stay put." Trent slams the door shut, leaving me feeling all alone for the first time in days.

"Turn on the damn light!" I yell to no one. Great. Now I am sitting in the middle of a dirty fucking bed with who the hell knows what on this floor. I curve my body around, placing my feet on God only knows what. However, as I start to walk with my hands out trying to find the wall in hopes the light switch is by the door, I am assaulted with carpet. It feels soft and squishy underneath my barely there flip-flops. Finding the door, I scrabble my way until I finally find a light switch. When I flick it on, I am stunned to silence by what I see before me.

"Holy shit."

There is a small, black-framed bed up against the wall, with a dark gray comforter and matching pillows, and a matching dresser, which I am currently propped up against. The room is spotless, except for the small amount of dust that has made its home on top of the dresser. The room is tiny, and as I take a few steps my mouth drops open and I collapse to the floor, gaping openly at the pictures above the bed and all across the entire length of the wall.

They are all of me. Me with Turner and my friends and family. Years . . . there are *years* of me in these pictures. I place my hand over my mouth to stifle my choking sobs as I try and gain some sort of composure and stand. Here is the proof of his obsession. Dear God, what is going on?

The walls start to close in on me as my eyes drop to a certain picture of Turner and me. This was right before he boarded that plane to take off for his business meeting. I reach for it and run my hands across Turner's face. In the picture, he has his hand on the back of my neck, bending down to kiss me goodbye. I pluck the picture off of the wall and bring it to my chest, placing it directly across my heart. Then I cry in absolute silence for what feels like eternity.

My husband is right across the hall from me and I can't even get to him. I am so afraid that he is really dead, or lying there badly injured. He must be. If something wasn't wrong with him, there is no way Turner would have heard me screaming for him and not tried to get to me. I just have to find a way to get to him.

Knowing this is Trent's room, I scan my prison looking for some kind of weapon. Both of those men underestimate the power of the love I truly have for Turner if they think they can keep me locked up in here until he, they, or who the hell ever decides my fate. Turner may never forgive me or want a damn thing to do with me after he finds out the debauchery I have sunk to with Trent; I can live with that, but what I cannot live with is not doing everything in my power to get him the hell out of here.

No sooner than I find what could possibly be a knife on top of the small dresser, I hear a key being turned in the lock. I shove the picture into my back pocket, realizing I have no time to grab the knife. I hear a rush of blood in my ears from my heart pumping overtime as the door slowly creaks open. I slide down the wall until my butt hits the floor.

Trent enters the room and follows the trail from the pictures to me sitting on the floor with his eyes. It's in that moment I fear for my life as he stands there with a smile, holding a gun in his hands. When he lifts it in my direction I try and scream, but nothing comes out. Nothing comes out at all.

The world goes black.

Chapter Twenty-Three

My head is killing me. Rubbing my temples slowly does no good. I know I am making some sort of whimpering sound. I am so sick and tired of being a punching bag for these psychotic fuckers. It's not until I open my eyes and I am lying in pitch darkness that I recall how I got here.

Trent. Everything leads back to Trent. He pointed a gun in my direction and I don't remember much after that. I'm alive. This much I know because I can feel the weight of his arm across me, and the smell of his alcohol on his breath. Unless I am actually in hell and he is here with me? Wouldn't that be my luck? Oh, yeah, how could I forget? I have been living in hell for days, now.

I chuckle at that thought, which makes him stir and I instantly go stiff. Please don't wake up. The longer you sleep, the longer I can try and make a plan to get the hell out of here. I lay there in silence as he rolls over to his other side and continues his snorefest. He's a freak. A crazy stalker freak is what he is.

It has to be sometime in the middle of the night and everyone is asleep; at least I hope they are. As drunk as his dad was earlier he has to be passed out somewhere in this shit hole, which gives me the perfect opportunity to try and get to Turner.

I carefully ease myself up and off of the bed and tiptoe as noiselessly across the floor as I can. The door handle turns with no difficulty at all as I open it and step out into the hall. My heart starts to beat rapidly as I stand staring at the door where Turner is. A small light is on in the living room and I hear heavy snoring coming from James, who must be on the couch.

Two steps, just two small steps bring me to the door. In silence I turn the doorknob just knowing it's going to be locked and all of my hopes dashed. I am stunned when it turns effortlessly and push the door all the way open, only to find myself staring at the silhouette of a body lying on top of a bed.

The room reeks of blood and urine. Only the thought of my husband lying there on that bed in whatever condition he is in keeps me from vomiting all over the place. I steady my unstable feet and press forward until I am standing directly beside him. It's so dark that it is nearly impossible for me to see, but I know it's him.

His breathing is somewhat erratic as if he is fighting to draw even a minimal amount of air into his lungs. Seeing him like this makes me want to go on a killing spree and murder both of these slimy bastards for hurting my husband. There really are no words to describe what they have done to him.

I don't have the time to stand here and think about torturing these men. I need to do everything I can to get my husband out of here and get him to the closet hospital. After what I saw earlier in Trent's room and how truly he is fixated on me, I trust him about as far as I can spit. He wants me for himself. And that right there is the reason why he's lying through his teeth. He thinks I'm a damn fool who believes he will truly help me. He's a damn liar and this is just as much his fault as it is his father's, as far as I'm concerned.

As I reach forward to touch him, Turner startles me as I hear my name come out of his mouth in a soft, hushed voice dripping with pain.

"Turner," I whisper.

I stand there and wait for a few beats and nothing. Is he talking in his sleep and only wishing I was here, or can he feel my presence just as I could feel he was near earlier? I don't know, but I am not going to think about that right now. I need to see if he is hurt badly in any way and if he is capable of getting up and walking so we can try and get out of here. It's our only chance right now.

I sit down beside him on the edge of the bed and reach out to stroke his hair. He's so hot to the touch when my hands finally make contact with his skin. He's burning up. Bile rises to my throat as I sit here in stunned silence taking in his beaten and bloody face. I cannot hold it in anymore. I stand and gag, ejecting the few contents of my stomach. The stench from this room does nothing but make it worse as my stomach clenches and I dry heave phlegm and spit. Swiping my mouth with the back of my hand, I turn back to my man, stroking his head comfortingly.

"God, baby. What have they done to you?"

"Clove? Is that you, or am I dreaming?" Turner asks softly. His voice is so hoarse and sounds like he hasn't had anything to drink for days. I'm so worried about what damage has been done to him. At last he's alive and he knows I am here.

"No, baby. It's really me."

"What are you doing here? H-how?"

"Shh. We can talk about all of that later. Right now I need to get you out of here. Can you get up and walk?"

"Honey, I don't know. My left leg is broken, and I am so weak. I have been beaten, and tortured, and-"

"Shh. I don't think I can take hearing everything they have done to you right now."

I continue to rub his head. I just can't keep my hands off of him. He's here and I have him and I cannot let him go again. I just can't.

"Turner, I have no plan. I don't know what to do, but we have to try and get out of here. Can you sit up?"

He moans as if he is in the most excruciating pain and my heart breaks as I hear him struggling to try and get up. His breathing raspy, he groans in anguish as he clutches hold of his stomach.

"H-help me baby."

His desperate words are almost inaudible. I do my best to try and help by guiding him up with my hands wrapped around his arm, but when he winces in pain I have no choice but to let go, fearful I will hurt him even more.

"Turner!" I half-sob.

"Clove, just give me a minute here. I need to sit up, and-*FUCK!*" he hisses as he pushes himself all the way up into a sitting position. All I want to do is kiss him senseless and hold him and take away every bit of pain he has. He's here. I am with him, and it kills me to not be able to hold him and to have his strong arms around me. There's just no time. Time is way too precious for both of us right now.

He struggles at his own pace until is able to swing his legs around. They drop with a loud thud to the floor. Time stands still and I stop breathing as my ears perk up. I glance at the open door, waiting and waiting for someone to walk in and hear us. When nothing happens, I reach out and place my hand over the top of his.

"I missed you so much," I say as I lean down and kiss his hand.

The waterworks start to flow hard and fast down my face, and before I know it I am quietly sobbing in his lap, clinging onto him as if my life depends on it. And he lets me. The irony of my life depending on him is all but hysterical since it's really the other way around. Saving both of our lives depends on me, not him.

My beautiful, strong man who has been to hell and back places his hand on top of my head and strokes my hair. His touch instantly soothes me. I dry the last of my tears with the backs of my hands and help myself up. Turner sighs and it's the most beautiful sound I think I have ever heard.

"You have no idea how much I missed you, either." My man is straining so greatly to even speak. "Everything about you gave me the strength to survive. I am so much in love with you, Clove Calloway."

He pauses.

"I'm a mess, my beautiful wife, but I need to feel your lips on mine more than I need to inhale my next breath."

Oh, God. I want that too, more than anything. When I lean in and our lips touch ever so tenderly, we both come undone. Our mouths open and our tongues glide over one another's in a kiss full of emotion. Love, hope, desperation, longing. Turner breaks our homecoming kiss recoiling in pain. I go to speak and he hushes me with a finger gently over my lips.

"How did you get here?" he whispers.

"Turner, we don't have time for any of that. We have to go now," I say urgently.

"I don't think I can walk, Clove. My broken leg is so swollen."

I shift my eyes to take a closer look at his leg, but it's so hard to see how much damage there truly is with the minimal light in the room.

"You should go and run. Run until you find someone to come back here."

Alarmed by his words, I jerk and shake my head back and forth.

"No! I won't leave you. I can't, Turner. I refuse."

"Fucking hell!" he cries out in agony, and I see his hand go to his side.

"What is it?"

My eyes desperately try to search his face in the faint light streaming in through the doorway. It's getting lighter by the second when I look towards the window and see outside.

"It's nothing, Clove."

He's lying. I know him.

"Baby, James is a crazy man. The thought of him touching even one hair on your gorgeous head would truly be the death of me. Please, just go. I love you too much to die. I can survive this as long as I know you will be by my side and in my arms where you belong when this is all over. Please don't fight me on this. Go, and get help."

I know he can see the despairing look on my face. He also knows I won't leave him as his brows furrow and he closes his eyes. And when he opens them I see and feel everything as our eyes tell each other how deep our love is.

"You are so damn beautiful."

He lifts his hands ever so carefully and cups my face. His hands are so rough, not smooth like they used to be, and yet I don't care. I sink into his touch. I feel it all the way into my bones and it's the best feeling in the world to finally be here with him. I keep my eyes closed for the longest time. I am so scared to open them and look at him. I know I am going to cry and lose it right here if I do.

I have to, though. I don't know if it's because I have to see him in the flesh to know he is really here with me, or if I need to look into his eyes and see the love I have missed so much shining brightly back at me one more time.

I open my eyes with my head bowed so that the first thing I notice isn't his face. I don't like what I see at all. Blood stained clothes. The same clothes he had on when he left for his trip. They're filthy and soaked in his own urine. Was he just thrown in here and left to try and survive on his own? And he looks so skinny.

After all he has been through, here he sits with his loving hand cupping my jaw and holding me as if I am everything to him. I make my weak self continue looking upward until I land on his jaw, which is now quite heavily covered with unshaven hair.

His face is swollen and his nose is crooked. He doesn't even look like the man I love at all, and yet when I reach those eyes of his, I smile when I see what I have been missing for over a week. I see my Turner.

The way he looks at me is like no other. It's the same look as I give him, the same look that has been staring back at me since the day I met him. It's the look of, *you're my forever, my one and only true love, and until my last breath I will cherish you always.*

Holes are being poked into my heart when I think about how much I have betrayed him, and on so many levels. As if he could read my mind, he bends down and places the lightest kiss on both sides of my cheeks.

"We will talk about everything later. Now let's get the hell out of here before-"

"Before what?"

We both turn our heads and James is standing in the doorway, hung over and waving a gun around in his hand.

"The two of you think you're going somewhere? Fuck that shit! The only place either one of you is going is six feet under and you, you fucking slut, are going first. I warned you not to cross me. It's because of you that I won't be getting what I fucking need to get me the hell out of this shithole. So you better say bye to my fucking pussy ass son because today is your last damn day on this earth."

He's dripping with such rage that I cower in front of Turner. Turner is weak and badly beaten; who knows how long he has gone without food or water? There is no way he can do anything to try and protect either one of us, even if he tried, so I can't afford to back down. I know it's crazy but I just can't stay and not fight for our lives.

"Listen, James. Why does it have to be this way? Why do you have to kill us both? I mean, I just don't get it. He's your son, for crying out loud! How could you do this to him? If money means this much to you, then we can get money for you. You don't have to kill us just because you can't get the money you thought you were going to get."

"Bitch, I know damn well you two don't have the kind of money I need. Do you think I am a fucking fool?"

"No we don't, but we know someone who does."

Turner winces in pain behind me and I turn to see he has fallen back down on the bed, barely able to keep his eyes open.

"Turner!" I turn to lean over him as his eyes roll into the back of his head.

"Turner, stay with me! Come on, baby!" I cry, shaking him ever so lightly.

"Babe, I would rather fucking die then to give that worthless fucker a dime," he groans.

"For the love of God, he's your son and he needs to get to a hospital. What kind of man are you to do this to your child?" I scream.

"I will tell you what kind of man I am, you fucking whore. I am a man who needs money; a man who thrives on inflicting pain on those I hate and I hate this son of a bitch who you call my son. He isn't my son. He's his momma's son. He's always been his momma's precious little baby boy. The one who couldn't walk or talk and cried like a fucking baby every MOTHER. FUCKING. DAY. My son is a man. Always has been since the day he was born and wrapped his fingers around my hand and gripped on tight, unlike this one here who screamed at the top of his lungs just begging to be held. Ain't no son of mine. Now let's talk about that money you said you could get me."

His tall and yet lanky frame comes into the room.

"Get the hell over here," he commands, lifting the gun in my direction.

"No!" Turner hollers from behind me. "Leave her alone. I know who she is talking about. Give me a damn phone and I will make it happen, but not until you let her go."

I shake my head no as I kneel down beside him on the bed.

"I am not leaving you. No way. Just let me make the phone call. I can do it from right here. I can't leave you now that I found you, Turner."

I hold his stare with mine even though he can barely keep his eyes open. He looks so much worse now that the weak early morning sunlight is cascading though the window. Bruises cover his face, neck, and bare arms. His striking green eyes are barely visible as he tries to hold them open.

Seeing exactly how badly Turner needs medical attention pushes me to the farthest point of my endurance, and I have had enough. Someway, somehow, I have got to get my bag out of that truck and get hold of the knife. A lot of good it's going to do me up against a gun, but it's the only choice I have, especially after last night's revelations about Trent.

"Just to be clear, love birds, no one is calling anyone. I know everything about the two of you. I know your brother is a detective and I would bet my life he's found a way to track your ass down by now. Ain't no damn way I believe a word your sweet little mouth says. Speaking of sweet little mouths . . . I do believe I need to sample what my offspring finds so delectable about you, don't cha think?"

Out and out horror pulses through my veins. My body shuts down and all I can feel are the tremors of the utmost fear imagining James touching me anywhere. Closing my eyes firmly, I try and re-group, telling myself to be strong. I don't open them until I hear Turner's words garbled in a painful jumbled mess from behind me.

"Y-you stay the fuck away from her, you worthless cocksucker."

James tilts his head and laughs, slapping his hands on his knees as if Turner just cracked some sort of funny joke.

"That's priceless, boy, coming from you. From where I stand, there isn't a damn thing you can do about it. Your punk ass is lying there half-dead. Your sweet little innocent angel here ain't so sweet anymore, are you sunshine?"

I'm stricken dumb. He really is a psychopath. My body goes rigid as I whirl around to gauge Turner's expression upon hearing this revelation. He's out cold and barely breathing as I watch his chest move up and down little by little.

"Turner, baby!"

I barely even touch him before James' next words cause me to jump out of my skin.

"Now, time to say goodbye, so I reckon you better get your ass over here, girl, unless you want me to finish him off right now."

I press my hand as delicately as possible against Turner's cheek, holding it there for a few moments just welcoming any kind of contact with him at all. And when I am jerked away from him by my arm forcibly, Turner's eyes fly open as he tries to reach for me, but fails. A slew of curse words leave his mouth.

"You're going to rot in here, motherfucker, so say good bye to your lovely wife," he snarls as he pulls me through the door and slams it behind him.

"Trent! Get your motherfucking ass up now and help me get rid of this bitch. We have to get to Mexico today. Our time is up."

He gets to the door to Trent's room and I hear Trent mumble that he's getting up. Fuck him, the spineless prick. All this time he has lied to me. He said he would do anything to try and save us. He's just like his father. Worse, even. If this is my last day here, I will make sure he knows exactly how I feel about him.

"Get your slimy hands off of me, you nasty old bastard!"

I squirm and try to break free of his grip on my arm as he drags me ruthlessly down the short hallway.

"Fuck off, cunt."

He shoves me down on the couch with so much force that I smack my head against the wall. I cry out as loud as I can and scream. I am so sick of being shoved around. I hear Turner yelling from the other room for him to leave me alone.

"Trent, shut that motherfucker up!"

Please, no!

I am trapped here as this man stands over me with his wandering eyes looking like he wants to have his way with me. That is one thing that will never happen. He will definitely have to kill me first before I let him touch me the way he wants to.

I hear the door to Trent's room open and then the other one slam shut as I sit there shaking. James is still hovering with his gun pointed directly in my face. It gets eerily quiet for a few beats and then a gun goes off. I scream and jump and try to get up as I kick and claw trying to get to Turner.

"Noooooo! Oh, God. No! Turner!" I scream as regret, sadness, and anger ripple throughout my entire body.

I sink back into the couch, dazed. I don't want to live if he is dead. All these visions start running through my head of my husband lying there, bleeding to death. I didn't say 'I love you' when I was forced from his room. I want to die right along with him. I have nothing left. That was it. They have broken me and now I don't care what they do to me. All my fight is gone as I slump back in defeat and cry a loud, soul-piercing cry.

"Oh my God, he's gone! What have you people done?"

My hands go into my hair gripping it tightly as I tug and rock myself back and forth.

"God, why? Why?" I wail.

Then Trent kneels down in front of me and all I see is red. Everything he has done to my life since he walked off of that damn plane comes flashing before my eyes and I hate him. I hate him so bad that I lunge at him and grab him by the neck. We go tumbling backwards, knocking over the flimsy coffee table which splinters in half.

Trent lands on his back with me on top of him. It doesn't take much for him to get me to release my hold but not before I have clawed the hell out of him.

"Fucking hell, Clove! Settle down!"

He grabs me by my wrist and pushes me backwards slightly. The look in his eyes is the same look he has given me before. Blank and unreadable.

"You liar!" I scream. "You said you would help us get out of here, and you killed him! You killed my husband! I hate you more than I have ever hated anyone or anything in my life. I hope both of you are happy now, because-"

"Because what, princess?"

James is now up in my face. The smell of his body odor and breath make me gag and I do nothing to disguise it. Trent wrenches me into a standing position as James moves in closer.

"I said, because what?"

I feel spittle all over my face as he is standing not even an inch away from me. Trent is now behind me securely holding my hands together. I am trapped. Sandwiched between two of the world's biggest frauds, pretenders, fakes, murderers.

"You lose, you fucking deadbeat!" I spit back in James' face. "You come out of whole thing empty. You orchestrated a senseless crime in hopes of getting your hands on money that never belonged to you in the first place. You're lower than scum and you will pay for what you have done and in the worst way."

I fling my hatred at him, and then I spit right in his face. I watch him stand there as his eyes change from mad to downright furious.

"You got a lot more heat and determination in you than what your husband had, I'll give you credit for that. But before I put a bullet through that pretty head of yours, I am going to fuck every hole in your body."

I feel Trent clench at his dad's words.

"Take her into your room and tie her up, then go into town and get me some coffee. I have a raging headache and this bitch is making it worse, boy. I ain't fucking around with this cunt anymore, or you either. You better have killed your sack of shit brother, boy, or I swear to God I will tie you up by your balls and beat you to fucking death."

Trent stands still for several heartbeats and says not a word as his father threatens him. Jesus, he is either brainwashed or scared of this man; most likely both. Well, I have a few words for this coward when we get alone, too. I know now that no matter what I say or try to do neither one of these two will listen to me, but I will not die before I make sure every word I have to say penetrates and wounds Trent in any way I can.

I let my head sag down, pretending to claim defeat as Trent brushes us both beside his father in a hurry and scuttles us down the hall toward his room. I close my eyes and desperately try not to open them as I know my husband's dead body is directly across the hall. He shoves me inside brutally hard after opening the door, and slams it shut behind him.

"Get on the bed," he demands.

"Fuck off! I will not get on that bed, you lying asshole!"

"Clove. *Get on the bed.* The longer you stand here and argue with me, the longer it takes for me to save you."

He's lying. Every fucking word he has ever said has been nothing but a damn lie. My life has been nothing but a fucking game of whiplash right to the fucking core.

"Since you stole my husband's life right out from under him, your warped mind thinks you can make me fall in love with you? Man the fuck up, Trent. Your father is a fucking chicken shit son of a bitch who has manipulated you your entire life. He has robbed you of a good home, a kind mother, and one hell of a brother who would have done anything for you if he would have known about you. And this is how you have repaid them both, by killing him at your father's command. And now you say you want to save me?"

I laugh.

"You want to save me, huh?" My finger pokes him in the center of his chest as tears of heartbreak roll down my face. "You just killed my husband, so there is no saving me."

"I didn't shoot him," Trent whispers.

It takes me a moment for my brain to register what he just said. And I don't believe him for one second. My sobs are uncontrollable now as I grieve the loss of the only man I have ever loved.

"You really expect me to believe you when all you have done is deceive me from day one?"

Tears are streaming down my face. My heart has been ripped out of my chest and I can't breathe.

"Just kill me, please. I beg you. I can't take this anymore," I plead, dropping to my knees.

"You have no reason whatsoever to believe me, Clove. I am telling you the God's honest truth here. I did not kill him." I study him closely as he stands before me with determination written all over his face.

"But I heard the gun!" I cry.

"Yes, you heard a gun, but I didn't shoot him. I opened the window and fired a shot outside. Now pull your shit together and listen."

I sit there and search his face trying to decipher if he is lying or not. This man before me lies so much I don't know whether this is a lie as well or if it's just another ploy to get me to be quiet. I have no other choice but to believe him, or at least pretend to.

"Now I am not going to tie you up. But you will sit on this bed until I come back."

"No! You can't leave me here with him. You heard what he said out there; he's going to rape me and then kill me."

My mind flashes back to yesterday remembering exactly what Trent did to me. I scurry back away from him until my back hits the wall. I see it clear as day that he is remembering what he did to me, too. Good.

"Fuck." He runs his hands through his hair and starts to pace the floor. "Listen to me for one goddamn minute. I am not leaving you for more than five minutes, I swear it. I am going to go out there and get into my truck and pull down the drive until he thinks I am gone. Then I am going to come back and tap on the window and get you out of here. We're both getting out of here."

"No! I am not leaving without Turner. He needs to get to a hospital before he really does die. Besides, what reason do I have to believe you anyway? You came in here last night and hit me with your gun. Why? Why would you do that?"

I plead with my eyes for him to give me an honest to God answer for once. Finally, he sighs.

"Fuck, Clove. He was ready to come in here and do all kinds of sick and twisted things to you. So I sat with him and made up all kinds of bullshit about how I would come in here and make you pay myself. He was so drunk when we got here he could hardly stand up straight, but when he got up and said he was coming in here to finish you off, I told him to wait and that I wanted you one more time."

He rakes his hands through his hair.

"When I came in here, I knew by the look on your face that you had seen all of the pictures of you all over the place. You're a feisty one, Clove, and I knew you would panic and start throwing your sassy mouth all over the place. So yes, I hit you. I am sorry for it, but I had to because it was the only thing I could think of to do at the time to save you from the sadistic things my father would have done to you."

Even though his voice sounds sincere, I'm not buying a word of it. Not one fucking word. Trent Calloway was sewn from the same damn cloth as his father, and in my judgment of character, he's the spawn of Satan himself. I will play along, though, until I get the chance to slice his fucking throat.

"Hurry the hell up and get me out of here."

Chapter Twenty-Four

I cannot hear a damn thing as I press my ear to the door and try and listen. Trent made me lock it from the inside just in case his dad tries to come in. It's not going to do me any good if he shoots a damn hole in it, but it will buy us some time. Yeah, you assholes. I am going to find a way to kill you both.

All I can think about is getting to Turner and killing these two cockroaches. God, I wish I had that knife right now. What the hell am I going to do? I am helpless and defenseless here.

I want so badly to walk across the hall to check on Turner and make sure he really is alive, yet here I stand docilely waiting for the man I hate. Believing in him and trusting him with our lives. I laugh out loud at that thought and how crazy it sounds.

I turn and press my body up against the door and sink to the floor. I keep my eyes trained on the window that is now wide open. The warm summer air is blowing through and I welcome it as I start to get impatient waiting for Trent. I keep a close watch on the alarm clock sitting on the small nightstand next to his bed. It's been eleven minutes now since he walked out of this room.

The doorknob jiggles and I hear the keys jingling in the lock. I stand up and my eyes go wide as I keep them glued to the door. Quickly, I scan the room for some kind of weapon to protect myself, but there is nothing. This room is spotless. I don't even see anything I could use as a weapon until my eyes land on a row of metal coat hangers hanging lazily in the small closet.

"I am coming for you, bitch."

The sound of James' voice makes me move my feet and I am grabbing a coat hanger off of the rod in no time. The door swings open just as I tuck the hanger behind me out of sight.

The bastard actually licks his lips as he saunters over to me and grabs me by my hair, and then flings me helplessly onto the floor. I somehow manage to keep my hand behind my back as I lay on my side, trembling.

"Where's Trent?"

"Don't worry about Trent. He ain't coming back for you, girl. In fact, he ain't coming back at all. Fine by me. Now I'm going to taste exactly what my boy seems to be infatuated with."

He tries to kick me over onto my back, but I don't budge.

"What do you m-mean, he isn't coming back?"

I'm trying to rein in my fear. James starts to laugh, but then his expression contorts from laughter to pain etched across his face. He looks straight at me and then it hits me as I cower.

"Oh my God! You killed him, didn't you? You killed your own son?"

He doesn't have to answer me; I can see it in his eyes. Oh, no. Even though I hated Trent, I feel as if his death is on my own hands because he was leaving to try and save my life and ended up being murdered at the hands of his own father.

"You don't think I knew about my son's infatuation with you? Look at that damn shrine on the wall over there." He extends his hand out in the direction of the wall.

"I told him over and over again not to fall for you, that all women are fucking whores and that is the only thing any of you are good for. Some of you aren't even good for that. But did he listen to me? Fuck, no. Fell for you the first time he laid his fucking eyes on you. You must be one good fuck there, bitch, to get both of my sons to fall in love with you. It's about time I see what that pussy of yours has that no other slut does, because it must be damn good."

He scans me up and down and lingers his eyes a little too long at my core.

"You sick man! You will have to kill me before I ever let you get your hands on me."

My words result in a slap across the face. I have had enough of being slapped and punched by men to last me a lifetime and I writhe along the floor trying to escape him.

"Where the hell do you think you're going?"

My resistance seems to appeal to him as he squats down and grabs hold of my face.

"I like em when they fight. Makes me want you all the more."

He grabs a handful of my hair and drags me a few feet. Before I have the chance to try and do anything with the hanger, he has me on my back with my hand securely underneath me as he straddles me. He starts ripping at my shirt while holding me down with his other hand wrapped securely around my neck, making it hard to breathe. His fingers dig into the already tender flesh. I am kicking and clawing at his face with my nails, tearing into his flesh. His face twists and he grimaces in pain as blood starts to trickle down his cheek. H lets go of his grip around my neck.

"You fucking worthless bitch!"

He shoves his gun against my temple, and the world stands still for me as I hear the click of a bullet being loaded into the chamber.

"You can fight me all you want, but I am getting what I came in here for. The more you fight me the better I like it. Now get up. Your life will end when and where I say it does, and it sure as hell won't be in this fucking room."

I don't care if me fighting him makes him angrier or turns him on. I am not getting up. I already know I am a dead woman, with Turner behind a locked door severely beaten and unable to even move, and Trent somewhere dead.

"You want to go the hard way then, huh? Well, let's go. The quicker I fuck you and kill you, the quicker I can get the hell out of here before your fucking family finds you. Though I would love to be here and see their looks of horror when they discover your beautiful face all mangled and beaten and your body sliced all the way from your pussy to your neck. Hell, maybe I will even cut you up into little pieces and throw them all over the place. That might be fun, too."

He's becoming more enraged by the second and yet I refuse to budge. That doesn't stop him from grabbing my legs and dragging me across the room as the carpet brushes roughly across my back, burning me.

It's so hard to act rationally when you are being attacked. The minute we enter the small hallway and he is pulling me past the room where I know Turner is, I scream. An ear-piercing scream of fear and dread as I swing out my hands and grab the doorframe.

"Turner! If you can hear me at all, please remember always how much I love you!" I yell with panic ripping through my body as James struggles to yank me forward and I hang on with determination.

My hands and fingers are slowly giving out against the strength of my attacker. He is grunting as he tugs and pain shears though my arms and legs as I let go. He drags me just a few more feet before dropping my legs and towering over me.

"Bitch! You need to be taught a lesson! You want to fight me all the way, then fine, because right here is where I am going to end your life," he sneers and lowers himself right onto my stomach, knocking all the wind completely out of me.

I am trying to gasp for air and every time I take a breath I inhale the reeking, disgusting odor of this man. It's enough to make me gag and cough as I feel like I am choking on my own bile. He doesn't care, though, as he slaps me in the face over and over again. I screech and try to block his blows with my hands covering my face as he continues to pound away at me.

"You have ruined my entire plan, you fucking bitch, and you are going to die! Do you hear me? I am going to kill you, Clove! Kill you with my bare hands, and after I am sure you are good and dead I am going to burn this fucking place down with the three of you in it!"

His face is red from his rage. All I can think about is wishing I still had that coat hanger in my hand. I can see it not far from where we are. I know I can reach it if I can just move six short inches, so I start to squirm and kick and do everything in my power to move my body closer.

James is still slapping me like a bitch and I am taking every blow and losing the strength to press forward. I keep repeating to myself, 'I can do this' as every blow seems to hurt less as my face grows numb. Blood is dripping down into my mouth and I know if I don't get to that hanger within the next few seconds, I am going to be out cold. All of a sudden he stops and his gaze follows my hand as I reach for the hanger.

"Fucking cunt!" he bellows loudly. "You can't outsmart me. You really must have me pegged for a fool."

He pulls his gun out from the back of his pants and shoves it into my mouth. My eyes go wide and I know any minute he is going to pull the trigger. I whimper in protest.

"That's what I thought." He leans in and starts kissing my cheeks. "It's too bad this pretty little face had to end up this way. Such a mess you are, Clove. I give you a shit ton of credit for trying to fight me, but the game is over, starting now."

He removes the gun from my mouth and places it back into the waistband of his pants. I can't move and I can barely see through my swollen eyes, but I do feel him shift his body slightly lower until his hands rest on my lower abdomen.

"Give up, Clove. I have you right where I want you. You can't escape. It's no use. There isn't anyone alive in here but me and you, and soon you will be dead, too. Now, I am going to take, and you're going to give."

I have no fight left in me as I feel him undo my jeans and yank my pants down. But then, I hear words from directly behind me. Words coming from a voice I recognize so well.

"Get off of my wife."

James' hands stop in midair as he looks up and his face shows stunned disbelief.

"I won't say it again. Get off of her."

Turner's voice is welcome to my ears, even though he sounds so weak and fragile.

"Fucking hell, boy. I should have known your brother wouldn't kill you like he was told."

James stands and straightens to his full height.

Slowly I get up and pull my pants back on in slow motion as I turn to look at Turner standing up against the wall with a gun pointed shakily in James' direction.

"You can't pull that trigger, you're too much of a fucking pussy to do it, aren't you Momma's boy? Always the one who could never do a damn thing for himself, ain't I right, boy?" he taunts.

"No, DAD. You're not."

And then the gun goes off as I turn from Turner to James and watch him stumble backwards. He manages to stay upright until the next bullet hits him square between the eyes. A shocked expression remains on his face as he crumples to the floor with a thud.

I stand there with my mouth hanging open for several beats. I turn to Turner with relief, wanting to wrap him in my arms and just hold him for a moment to celebrate that our nightmare is over. But before I can even take one step toward him, the roar of another gunshot slices through the air and Turner slumps to the floor at my feet.

"NOOOOOO!"

I throw myself down beside him as he lies on his side, bleeding from a wound in his chest. He reaches out weakly and grabs my hand.

"G-get out of here. Call for h-help."

He can barely get the words out and his eyes flutter closed and then open again.

"No! I can't leave you like this. Can you get up?" I whisper.

"I don't think I can, baby. I d-don't think I am going to make it."

His eyes drift closed again and this time they don't open back up. I start shaking him and screaming at him to wake up, my tears flowing like a river dripping down onto his face. He's limp and lifeless lying before me.

"He's dead, Clove."

I hear a sound coming from the shadows in the other room. I must be going crazy. I look up and there standing before me with a gun in his hands is Trent. What in the motherfucking hell is going on?

"Trent. I . . . he . . . he said you were dead! Your dad said he killed you!"

What the hell is happening here? I don't know how to react or what to do. My husband is dead? God, no. He's not. I refuse to believe it, and yet I cannot seem to lift my head or open my eyes. I don't even remember closing them.

"Clove."

I feel Trent's cold, clammy hands rest on my arms and I scream, crawling into the corner of the hallway. I pull myself up on legs that feel like rubber as he moves closer to me and boxes me in, pinning me with his glare.

Time freezes for one fleeting moment and everything that has happened to me comes back in a flash of agonizing reality. This brutal son of a bitch has flipped my world into a deep abyss of darkness.

I let out a growl. He played me. This motherfucker played me again. Rage builds up inside of me and I push him as hard as I can. I watch him stumble backwards and grasp the side of the wall to keep him from falling.

"WHAT HAVE YOU DONE?" I point my finger to the floor at my husband's body lying there, still not able to look at him. Tears stream down my face and what pieces of my heart were left are broken when I truly realize that Turner took his last breath saving my life.

"He was in the way of me and you. I had to shoot him, Clove. I had to."

Trent's lips tilt up into an amused smirk, bitterness dripping from his words like the sound of pouring rain.

"You motherfucker! I told you I will never be with you. EVER! You're a liar and a thief and now you have murdered the man I love, and yet somewhere in your sick, perverted head you still think I want to be with you? Fuck you! I will never be with you. I will never love you. You mean nothing to me. Do you hear me? NOTHING!"

I don't want to be here in this life anymore. The smell of blood assaults my nostrils at next intake of breath from the puddles of blood by both Turner and James. Red. I see red as I look to the floor one last time and I know now what I am going to do as I see my love and his life that was ended way before it should have been. The one man I ever loved is gone and the man I hate is now beside me extending his hand to me.

I just don't know what the hell is happening here. I thought Trent was dead and I put all the energy I had left into either killing or hurting James badly enough to be able to escape. Now I have nothing left. Absolutely nothing at all as I see Trent's hand begging me to come to him.

"You're coming with me," he says before I collapse to the floor.

I shake my head 'no' as he moves closer to me. I reach out my hand and my fingers close around the coat hanger I took from his room.

"I will not live my life in hell or with a man who took my husband's life. You've lived in hell your entire life, and my guess is you love it there. So while I spend eternity with my husband, I hope you rot in hell, and it's the worst type of pain to ever be inflicted on your blackened soul."

I twist open the top half of the hanger and the last words that come out of my mouth before Trent can make it to me on time are,

"FUCK YOU."

And I plunge the end of the hanger straight through my broken heart.

Epilogue

I wake up screaming wildly and bolt upright in bed, thrashing around violently as if I am trying to protect myself. It's daylight and the sun is shining through the blinds as my eyes dart around my bedroom.

"Oh my God. I am in my room. This can't be. How did I get here?"

My hands start frantically touching and pinching at my skin to see if I am dreaming. I'm not. I really am in my bed. Did I survive? There is no way I could have. I killed myself in order to be with Turner. I try and bring my knees up to my chest and they barely move. Am I paralyzed now? And why is the bed all wet underneath me? Flipping off the covers in a hurry, I stare down in shock as my eyes land on my very large, pregnant belly.

I don't know how to explain this. Did I dream the entire thing? Am I hallucinating? How long have I been like this? My eyes scan the spot next to me in bed and I am alone. I need to get up and call my brother and find out what the hell is going on. Just as I swing my legs over the side, I hear footsteps charging up the stairs. I stand and turn toward the door and when he walks through the door, I scream.

"Clove, baby. I heard you screaming. Are you all right? Did you have another nightmare?"

My mind is telling my body that I should fear this man and yet my heart is telling me to run to him.

"Who are you?" I whisper.

He cocks his head as if my words have stunned him

"What do you mean, who am I? Did you have another nightmare, honey?" he asks as he moves closer.

My legs have turned into a solid brick of ice and I cannot move as he stands in front of me and places my hand in his. His hand is comforting and smooth and something about it just feels so right.

"Turner?" I utter in confusion.

"Yeah, it's me, Clove. Did you have another nightmare?" he asks again as he takes both hands and rubs them up and down my arms in the gentlest way.

"A nightmare?" My mind is a muddled and tangled up mess.

"Yes, you've been having those a lot lately as we get closer to your delivery date."

Did I just hear him right? A baby? Our baby? No, this can't be true. He can't be alive. He can't be real.

I reach out and grasp his face with my hands and search deep within his eyes to see if he is real. And he is. He's real. Turner is alive and it was all a nightmare! A terrible, horrible dream. I bring myself closer to him and watch his lips part as if he is expecting the kiss I so urgently want. The mouth that always soothes and consumes me. Or is it? This crazy, fucked up, twisted mind of mine has to know, and there is only one way to find out.

Slowly, with shaky hands, I unbutton my dress, exposing my swelled breasts.

"What are you doing?"

The sound of his voice has me swallowing, scared as a mouse trapped in a corner with nowhere to go as the cat slinks its way toward its prey, back hunched, ready to attack. Closing my eyes, praying, hoping, and wishing, at first I don't see what it is I am looking for. But when I open them, I let out a blood-curling scream. There, centered just above my breast, is the scar. The scar left by the hanger I stabbed myself with.

The baby decides to kick hard at this precise moment, bringing me to my knees. The fear, the agony. It wasn't a dream at all. Why did I survive? How? A sharp pain rips through my stomach as it tightens and I double over, my hands bracing against the floor in front of me.

I look up bitterly at my betrayer . . . a killer, and God forbid, the father of my unborn child. The man standing in front of me isn't Turner, and this wasn't a nightmare at all. This is reality, and this is hell, because this man is Trent. Slowly I shake my head back and forth.

"Y-you won, Trent. Didn't you?"

The darkness continues to devour my tortured soul.

Acknowledgements

Tony, my one true love. You swept me off my feet twenty-two years ago when my eyes first landed on yours the minute you stepped through the door of that bar. My feet never once touched the ground again. The world will now know it was love at first sight.

My boys, Aaron and Shane. You call me the best word ever created: MOM.

Mom and Dad. You always encouraged all seven of us to follow our dreams. I'm living proof that dreams really do come true.

Margaret McHeyzer. You, my friend, were one of the first authors to tell me I could do it. You have helped me more than anyone. One of these days I will come face to face with you, and when I do, be ready for this old lady to leap into your arms. Thank you!

All of my author buddies. You know who you are. Your friendship means the world to me. EVERY SINGLE ONE OF YOU.

My friends and cover models, Tessi Conquest and Nathan Weller. I have no clue where to even begin with the two of you. God placed the three of us together for a reason. Not too many people have the type of bond we do. My love for you grows every day.

My BETA readers. You make me shine bright in this world. You dedicate so much of your time to me. True friendship is what I feel for you. Thank you for being on my side.

My Krew. What can I say, except for the fact I would be nothing without all of you. I have never seen a group of women work as hard as all of you. Lip smacking face kisses from me to you.

Kimberly Capuccio, my editor. Book three, baby! Many more to come for me and you. Words cannot even begin to express my gratitude to you. My love can, though, and you have it. If someone were to ask me right this very minute the one person I want to meet most in this world, it would be you. That day is coming my lovely lady, and my arms are open wide.

To My Author buddies in TGNAFN. Our daily chats and loyalty and trust towards one another are sacred.

My girl Chelle Bliss. I think the entire reading world knows what you mean to me. I will always have your back.

Eric David Battershell. You just needed to go in here. Why? Simply because you came into my life just when I needed a friend, and now our friendship will last forever.

Every reader, blogger, photographer, model. The list is endless when it comes to you. Thank you for taking the time to read my stories and to send me messages with kind and caring words. I never take anyone or anything for granted. Know this from the depths of my soul- I adore you.

My dreams have only just begun; live yours, make them happen. You have the ability to do so.

Contrite Playlist

4 Non Blondes- What's Up
ZZ Ward- Put the Gun Down
Kenny Wayne Shepherd- Blue on Black
Melissa Etheridge- Come to My Window
REO Speedwagon- Ridin'the Storm Out
Buckcherry- Sorry
George Michael- I Want Your Sex
Pat Benatar- All Fired Up
Leona Lewis- Bleeding Love
Kelly Clarkson- Stronger
Natasha Bedingfield- Unwritten
Alicia Keys- No One
P!nk- Try